MARISSA RIVERA

My Name is Scream

First published by SteffyInk Publishing 2023

Copyright © 2023 by Marissa Rivera

All rights reserved. No part of this publication may be reproduced, stored or transmitted in any form or by any means, electronic, mechanical, photocopying, recording, scanning, or otherwise without written permission from the publisher. It is illegal to copy this book, post it to a website, or distribute it by any other means without permission.

This novel is entirely a work of fiction. The names, characters and incidents portrayed in it are the work of the author's imagination. Any resemblance to actual persons, living or dead, events or localities is entirely coincidental.

Marissa Rivera asserts the moral right to be identified as the author of this work.

First edition

ISBN: 978-1-7373355-3-5

This book was professionally typeset on Reedsy. Find out more at reedsy.com

A message from the Author:

This book deals with heavy themes such as human trafficking, suicide, murder, domestic abuse, and R-rated language. The writing accommodates to Young Adult audiences to bring awareness to these themes. And though it is a dystopian Society, these themes are happening in our world to kids, teens, and adults on a daily basis.
Read with caution and with the permission of an adult.

This book is dedicated to dreams.
Whatever they are, follow them.

Acknowledgement

This book has been in my heart and on my computer for nearly ten years. It has gone through a huge overhaul a dozen times. And just like me, it has come out better than ever. I'm proud of this work and what it's become.

Thank you to my husband, Christian, who funds my creative mischief, not only with actual funds but with constant positive reinforcement, helping me reach my goals even when I'm struggling.

Thank you to my editor, Sariah, who saw the story's potential and helped mold it into what it is today.

Thank you to my ARC reviewers who give the best feedback.

Thank you to my mother. She died three years ago battling colon cancer. She gave me my first laptop at fifteen and I haven't stopped writing since. She always knew I'd become an author and encouraged my writing from the very beginning.

1

Welcome to Myers' School For the Unwanted

Rule One: Do Not Attempt Escape

They cut the rope from my wrists. I don't move, appearing dead, wishing I was. I fought as best as I could, but three against one is never good odds. I wonder if I should give up and lay here until the buzzards peck at my skin and rip me apart one limb at a time.

Long, spiny fingers grip my neck, lifting me. I bring my gaze to the boy's face. In the shadows, he has devil horns and sharp teeth, inhuman in every possible way. But he shifts, and a distant light illuminates his face exposing an ordinary teenage boy with dyed white hair and brown eyes.

"Tell Tobias we aren't gonna stop."

"Tell him yourself." With my last ounce of strength, I swing my hand up, digging my nails into his cheek.

He drops me, stumbling back, holding his bleeding face. Rage ignites in his eyes. He grabs the knife at his boot and the metal flashes from the lamp.

His two buddies grip his arms, "Cloud, no." They remind

him he isn't allowed to kill me. I lay there watching a bull buck behind a cage. It's satisfying to know even clan members are scared to break the rules.

Cloud breaks from their hold, and slips the knife back in his boot. He touches his cheek, eyeing the blood on the tips of his fingers before he points at me, "One day, Scream, the clans are gonna decide they don't want you here. And I hope I'm around to see it."

The three boys head out for the exit, leaving me behind like garbage. I study their shadows as they glide across the football field till they disappear beneath the bleachers. They must have watched me enter the secret entrance. I'm so stupid for not noticing them.

Where had they hidden?

I suppose it doesn't matter. I won't make the same mistake twice. I'll have to find somewhere else to go but for now I'm too tired to move. I'm shivering under the desert night sky, the stars bright and plentiful, watching me from afar. The sandy floor does nothing for warmth but there's no point in leaving. The morning will rise soon enough, and I'll have lived another day inside Myers' School for the Unwanted.

As the sky brightens, the clouds roll by.

It's peaceful. It's deceiving.

For a few moments, I can imagine I'm somewhere else, somewhere safe, somewhere not here.

Does a place like that exist?

With my bruised hands on the sandy floor, I push myself up. Moans of pain breach my cracked lips, and tears drip down my dirty cheeks. My jeans are ripped and dry blood hardens the fabric. My brown shirt stretches over my shoulder now from being pulled and yanked. I try to tighten it but it just falls over anyway. With my long hair tossed over my shoulder, I take a deep breath and cry out. The pain radiates from my ribs and I'm fearful something's broken. Like any animal in the wild, it's dangerous to have a weakness, and I can't be weak. I lift my shirt to find a massive black and blue welt expanding from my ribs down to my hip. My shaking fingers grace the discolored skin, but there's no telling if anything's fractured. It doesn't matter anyway. Medical help is only for the ones that can afford it.

And that's not me.

On my arm is a black ribbon. It fills me with bitterness, and I pull it, throw it, cursing it. The ribbon was supposed to stop people from attacking me. But last night, it was a calling card. Those boys targeted me because of who I know, not because of something I did. I wish that took away the shame, but it's still there because who I know is a piece of shit.

I stare at it on the sand, resenting the piece of fabric before I reach for it despite the agony it causes. I rewrap it around my arm.

Standing takes effort. My feet drag in the dirt. I spent too much energy fighting them off and without sleep, I can barely think but routine helps get me where I need to go.

Bathroom.

Shower.

Dress.

School.

On the outside of the football stadium, there is a square building for the locker room. Rain members are up early for their morning basketball game. As spectators, they stand around, talking. They wear unsullied clothes with blue and white colors that represent their clan. They look pristine with their washed skin and brushed hair. They laugh and smile, playing with each other, appearing as if they could do no evil.

Rule 16: The clan Rain will provide Food and Water for the Populace.

A white shirt, like the boy who attacked me. I close my eyes and see it. There was a tattoo on his neck, blood droplets falling from a cloud.

Cloud, they called him.

I slow my approach as I near the bathroom. Beside the building is an abused playground. Chains are broken, the paint is chipped and the slide has a hole in it. Bald headed Mine members hang like monkeys over the dilapidated swing set, eyeing the Rain members with cruel intentions. They aren't daring enough to attack a whole group so they lay in wait hoping one would stray off. A little boy watches me. The black ribbon protects from clans, not Rats or Mine members but thankfully there is nothing I possess that they want, so they smoke their cigarettes and ignore me as I limp by.

The girl's basketball team drifts in and out of the entrance to the locker room. They wear high top shoes, blue shorts and white shirts with their numbers. They are all tall and skinny with their hair pinned to their head. I wish I could have something like that, a scrunchy that I could wrap in my hair to keep its knotted tresses off my sweaty neck but I'm not allowed.

I enter the girls' side before another person. The Rain member looks back at me, shocked and somewhat concerned.

She must be new.

Her friend pulls her along, whispering, "That's a Rat. Don't look at it."

I lean against the wall. I'm a Rat, a kid that isn't a part of the clans. If I had been given a choice, I would have been in Rain. I hear they have big swimming pools in their building. I'd be swimming every day if only to get out of the constant heat.

Further in, the girls chatter like birds at a pool of water and it echoes in the showers. I lean against the wall and listen. A random conversation sounds like music. Their words aren't important. It's the sound alone that makes me feel included, belonging, like she's talking to me.

It's envy, what I feel. I've never had a friend or someone to eat with at lunch.

Tobias would never allow it.

The shower stalls are old, and like the playground, things are broken and the yellow paint on the walls disintegrates over time. The mirrors have never been cleaned and have a dust film over it. I've taken a towel once and twice if only to see my reflection but I'd rather not look at myself yet.

I strip and squeeze into a little, dirty cubicle. With a press of a button, a timer for three minutes begins. There's a dispenser of soap attached to the wall and luckily it's been full. Rain is responsible for the upkeep of this locker room but they don't put much effort into it.

I rush as I scrub my skin. I scrub around the welts, hissing when I run over one. The water is freezing and hits me like icicles. At my feet the water turns pink as all the wounds I've accrued open but eventually, it clears. It always clears. I watch it to remind myself of that. No matter how bad it gets, it's not forever.

The water snaps off as I rub off the last of the soap. There are no towels, so I stand in the stall, drip drying. As I step out, the mirror calls to me and I approach it slowly, unsurely.

Do I want to see?

With my wet hand, I wipe it across the panel.

A stranger stares back. Always a stranger. I have no memory of life outside the school. My first memory is waking up on a bus and being brought here. Everything of who I was before I came to this place is gone.

I step closer to the mirror, inspecting my face. I'm between fifteen and seventeen years old. I'm either white or Spanish considering my tan but I blame that on the ridiculous sunlight. I was born from someone. Did I call her mother? Was she pretty? Was my father strong? Someone brought me into this world, even if they didn't want me. They gave me pieces of themselves before they gave those pieces away.

A school for the Unwanted.

I shove myself forward. It isn't the time, and I've got to hurry. Pain is making me slow enough without my thoughts drifting. I snatch my clothes from the floor, but they are ripped and dirty. I don't want to put them back on, but I might not have an option. There are bins that used to be full of clothes, flip-flops, and random items. The clans have taken all of it to sell back to the populace. The only things that get replenished and remain free are disposable items like toothbrushes, dime-size toothpaste, antibacterial hand soap, and deodorant sample packs. There were little plastic combs, but there wasn't any left. I don't much care about the state of my wet hair, knotted and unkempt as it is.

As I'm brushing my teeth, I hear the bell ring. School is starting.

The girls are clearing out, and there is a slight chance they've left something behind. Anything is better than the clothes I have. Stealing from clan members means punishment, but I can't put on those wretched clothes without exploiting all options first.

I tiptoe around the bend, going to the front door and sticking my head out. They're heading to the field, far from me now. One person is left behind, lingering as they talk to the Mine members. Only a clan member would have the audacity to pay off those scrubby scavengers. I spin around and dart to the locker room.

They've left all of their stuff—bags full of clothes. I laugh but clamp a hand on my mouth.

What idiots! Are clan members so far removed from reality that they'd leave their stuff behind?

My heart thumps wildly in my chest, my eyes flipping madly about, wondering if it's a trap-if someone is in the corner somewhere waiting for me. I mosey around, peeking at every dark spot, but the room is empty.

My hand tentatively moves toward a bag. Inside are clothes, shoes, sports bras, deodorant, a makeup kit, and hair products.

I've hit the freaking jackpot.

My heart is racing. If I steal, I could be signing away my life. But what are a couple of items from hundreds? There's a chance they might not even notice. I should be okay if I take one piece of clothing from four bags. And how will they know it's me? Mine members can take the blame.

That girl at the entrance. She looked right at me.

But a shirt and a pair of pants shouldn't be missed. They'll never know.

Rule 13: Do Not Steal, Harm, or Lie to a Teacher or a Clan Member

I dig into a few bags, taking what I need, and slip them on quickly. A black shirt, gray slacks, and flip-flops are nothing to miss.

With the black ribbon tied around my arm, I look in the mirror, feeling more like myself, the 'me' I've become in the last few months. If I can make it through last night, I can make it through school.

Unless I get caught.

2

Class

Rule Two: All Students Must Go To School.

The school sits in the center of town like all the other buildings were built around it. It was the first thing I saw when I got here. The school is six stories and made of red brick. Every window is covered with metal bars, but I can't imagine anyone trying to break in.

Clan graffiti dominates the lower portion with curse words, clan symbols, and recruiting posters. Rain, Coal, and Boundary draw over each other's artwork like a desk with too many papers. Only one sign remains untouched: the rules of the school. It's not something we're allowed to forget. Even now, it plays over the intercom, a continuous monotonous sound, a male voice reciting all nineteen requirements.

Stairs lead up to the entrance, and I lean on the banister, wincing with each movement.

Packs of blue and white, red and yellow, and gray and black pass by me. Everyone is a part of some clique. Members are known for the colored clothes they wear. Some look at me, and I hesitate.

Rule 14: Do Not Pretend to be a Teacher or a Clan Member

My black shirt could be misconstrued for Coal, but without the symbol on the front, a skull head with a light on the forehead, I'm not falsifying my station.

As the second bell rings, students rush to their classrooms, fear increasing with every step. I take a deep breath and hurry, nearly crying by the time I get to the top. I glance around me, searching. I reach the doorway to my classroom as the bell rings, and out of the corner of my eye, I see her, a Respect Member with a baton in her hand. She gives me a fake smile and touches the black ribbon on her arm. I glance at mine, sickened by our connection.

It's the first day of new classes and I step into the classroom. There is nothing different about this room compared to the next. They are cookie cutter copies. A square full of desks for thirty students. At the head of the classroom is the teacher's elongated table, usually empty. Beside it hang a giant American flag, and a round black rimmed clock hung on the wall next to it. The Pledge of Allegiance outlines the room like wallpaper, repeating as it encircles us. Though I've read it many times, I'm still unsure what it means.

And like most of the corners in this school yard, a camera's red dot zooms in on me.

I move to a vacant seat, feeling the weight of a bunch of eyes on me. I keep my head down, trying to sink into the floor.

"Look, it's her," a whisper slips into my ear. I sit in the chair closest to the door for a quick escape. The less movement, the less they'll look at me. I try to maneuver in my chair in some way to sit without showing I'm hurt. But like a predator, they can sense the blood.

"I hear Rain went after Tobias last night."

"Looks like she got caught," they cackle like hyenas. "Guess she's not as fast as they say."

Miss Nancy walks in. She's panting and waddling, while her blond hair sticks to the back of her sweaty neck with the rest of it is in a skin pulling bun. She taps a pointer stick against the blackboard. "Quiet."

The response is instant, and no one dares to move. Rule three: Obey The Teachers is embedded into our heads like a tattoo.

"Peat, pass out the books."

A Coal member dressed in black from head to toe hops up, eager to do her bidding. He delivers each book to a desk until he gets to me. It falls to the floor, loud and shocking. Once more, the eyes of the students are on me. I grit my teeth and reach for it. The pain intensifies, and a tear pushes through, but I wipe it before anyone can see it.

"Page 86." She slaps a picture on the blackboard and pins it with a magnet. An ugly looking man with a thin mustache stares back with cold dead eyes.

"Hitler was a man of talented articulation. He could coerce millions of people to believe in his own philosophies. Believe so much in him to propel him toward total supremacy. What gives a single person so much power?" She waits for a response. "Fear," She smiles as if the word is joy on her lips. "A flip of a coin," she points to the crowd, "You would be dead. A wrong look," she points to another, "You would be dead." Miss Nancy leans against her desk. "They say people knew what was happening to the Jewish population, and no one did a thing to stop it. Why? Because they were afraid to speak.

"Hitler set out to eradicate a race of Jewish people because he believed he was better. Many liked him because of his ability to befriend and manipulate. And those that became his friends were given positions of power to make them feel special. They ruled over the Nazi party, which Hilter called his followers. They all used fear to remain in power." Miss Nancy pins another picture. It's a woman so deprived of food every bone in her body shows through her stretched skin. Most of her hair is gone, and pieces struggle to stay attached. She reaches out to the camera, her fingertips bitten off in moments of desperation. Her lips are gone as well as her tongue. "Fear makes you compliant. Fear makes you faithful."

Miss Nancy stands, putting on her glasses, using her stick to point to the first image. She can say all she wants about him but he's hideous. I wouldn't follow him for that alone.

"You and Hitler have something in common. You all have what out there would call 'an evil' inside you. A hatred so deep you can't be around normal people. Because you'll kill anyone that loves you," she pauses, leaning against her desk. "We took you because you are sick. We are not bad people. You are. You are here because your parents asked us to take you."

I hold my hands to my ears.

I'm not sick. I'm not bad.

"We want you to be who you are without being judged and hated. Out there, beyond those walls, no one wants you. No one loves you. You are too demented to be loved. But here, you are accepted. Your desires are welcome. Be who you are."

Her attention fastens on a student. A boy stands in front of his desk. He is clearly a Mine member with his shaved bald head and dirty clothes. He's young, around ten with a face of a tired old man.

"Memory says you're wrong," he says boldly.

The students are too awe-struck to behave, whispering and laughing. They all seem to know who Memory is while I'm left wondering. It hasn't been the first time I've heard their name, and sometimes, during the night, someone will spray paint their name on walls. But it never takes the clans too long to paint over it.

Miss Nancy chews the inside of her lip, a glare frozen with animosity. I catch his face again. He doesn't look down, and he doesn't give in. He's determined and fearless. "You stole us. You took us from our moms and dads who love us, and they are out there waiting for us to return. Memory is going to kill you," he bites. "She's going to save us."

Tobias said my parents are dead. But what if he lied?

"Save you?" the woman spits out. "Memory's dead. I wish I had put the bullet through her head." She spins to the button on the wall. "Ira," she speaks through the intercom.

"Yes, Miss Nancy?"

"Send someone down, please." She eyes the boy and says, "We have someone claiming Memory will save him."

The boy runs, hopping over chairs, desks, and children, grabbing the doorknob. The lock jerks, and he yanks and shoves, slamming his fist down on the knob. He should know by now they use deadbolts, I criticize. He shouldn't have spoken out. What is he trying to prove?

He hurries to the windows. Bars of steel wrap them tightly.

RULE ONE: Do Not Attempt Escape.

That's what they are really for. To keep us in, not to keep us out.

The door unlocks. The room is silent and still, holding its breath.

Stepping into the room is Tobias. As the Respect leader, he holds his back straight, with a leather whip dragging behind like Satan's tail. Tobias is an older teen covered in random tattoos. He has a shaved head with one long scar running up his chin, through the tip of his mouth, and up through his cheek, ending at the edge of his eye. He loves to show it off, so he unconsciously leans to the right, giving everyone a better look.

My body goes cold. The air is nearly impossible to breathe. I clench my desk, the only thing separating him and me. It's not enough. Miles and miles wouldn't be enough.

Since I first came here, Tobias took it upon himself to rule my world. And I have done all I can to expel him from it.

"Tobias," the boy pleads, approaching with desperation. "Memory is alive. You believe that, don't you?"

Without giving a response, Tobias stretches his arm behind him and slaps the whip down. I squeeze my eyes shut and with every hint I flinch. Blood splatters the walls, and the smell of bowels fills the room. It takes little time to destroy the confident boy who stood before Miss Nancy. It's a fleeting memory—a shooting star.

I dare to peek between my fingers. Tobias snags on to the boy's foot and drags the unconscious kid out. The lock clicks behind him.

Miss Nancy slaps her hands together like she wiping dust off her palms. "Guess Memory couldn't make it today." She opens the window to fan out the air. Her step is a little livelier and she hops over the streak of red paint on the floor.

And we all sat here.

Because of fear.

3

Caught

Six hours of listening to Miss Nancy drone on has me staring at the clock waiting for the final bell. When it happens, I let everyone else go first, unwilling to risk anyone in my personal space. I can't really get up that fast either. I feel like I've fallen down the stairs. Every inch of me hurts and it's exhausting.

I walk through the hallways with my head down, my knotted hair hiding my face. I ignore the kids looking my way or the whispers following me. They hate me because of Tobias but they fear him enough to stay away. I daydream about what life would be like here if I wasn't associated with a monster. But I'd probably chase people away regardless. I'm not exactly a perky person and I don't see myself chatting about the cutest boy in school.

"There she is."

I snap my head up. Rain's basketball team stands in front of me. Tall girls and boys glare at me in blue and white bound together like a rubber band.

It's not a time to panic. I search for an escape. I'm a fast runner, but their long legs might overcompensate my speed. And if one gets me, they all will. The black ribbon around my arm won't help me now. I've broken a rule.

I try to produce an excuse, my mouth falling open stupidly, but nothing comes out. Nosy students look on, blocking traffic, interested in what I've done now. I'm in too much pain to fight, and I lost my weapon last night. Fighting on school grounds has rules. No death. One-on-one only. I scan them to determine which ones I can win against.

A girl from the circle nastily shouts out, "You think you can steal from us because of who you are?"

Who am I?

My response is thoughtless, "It's your dumbass fault for leaving your shit behind."

Cackles and shocked 'oohs' surround me like a ring. I internally curse myself for my big mouth. It's one of my worst qualities.

She steps forward with balled fists, but her eyes snap behind me. The sudden quiet unnerves me, and I swing around, ready to fight, but even I can't move as Hail approaches.

Hail is the co-leader of Rain. He is slow, taking each step as if he doesn't really want to move. He keeps his hands in the pockets of his black cargo jeans, sloughing like gravity is too heavy for his tall frame. I stumble slightly backward as he comes near me. It's deceiving how he acts. I've seen him fight and there is nothing that holds him back.

Hail stops. For a moment, his brown eyes look at me until he flips his gaze over my head to his clanmates. Their energy dies down, and they shift uncomfortably under his scrutiny.

"Who attacked you last night?" he asks me while eyeing each person in the group.

I look out to the crowd and see Cloud standing in the back. Scratches mar his white face. He keeps back, sinking, but his beady eyes warn me, a promise of vengeance I wouldn't be able to stop.

"I don't know."

Hail takes a step forward, "Rain has a reputation of honesty, intelligence, and compassion. If you have a problem with another student, you come to me!" he barks suddenly, but his voice levels out again as if he's too tired to keep the momentum. "I want the names of members who attacked Tobias' clan last night by tonight, or there will be punishment." Hail looks back at me, "Go on now." I'm not sure what he means at first, and then he nudges his head, a silent demand. Unlike when Tobias orders me around, I have no problem obeying this time. I run out of the school entrance and don't look back.

I keep moving, even sluggishly, till I've climbed all the stairs to a Rat building. Six floors up, and I collapse. My body has given out and even breathing is difficult because with every inhale there's a stabbing pain in my side.

I'm so stupid. Why did I take these clothes? I almost got killed! I have to do better.

Survival is what matters. Clothes don't matter. A shower doesn't matter. Survival is the most important. I can't risk my life for stupid material things. It's not worth it.

That's the logical part of me but the child in me wants what the other kids have. I want clothes I didn't steal. I want a bed with fighting someone off. And food I didn't have to work for.

If Tobias didn't run my life, didn't ruin my chances of becoming a clan member, I could have it all. But how do I get out from under him?

Does it even matter? Why is survival important?

I have come back to this question too many times. I've begun to believe it's not going to get better. I thought someone would come along and save me. It was a naive hope, one created by a dream. But now, as the months have trickled on, no one is coming. There's nothing other than this world and trying to survive it.

So what's the point?

I sit up.

The Rat building is an ill-kept apartment. There are forty rooms, spaced out on six floors, all fit with a bathroom and kitchen. Whoever was building it decided to stop. The toilets don't work, and the rooms are half constructed. But it has a roof, and I come here when I'm desperate to get out of the rain. It's not, however, a safe place to sleep. Too many clan members come through here looking for fun.

My stomach rumbles. I didn't get breakfast this morning, and I'm starving. I could go straight to the Cafe and get the free goop they provide, but I'd rather have something tasteful.

First, I need money. My chosen occupation is not a popular one, but it's away from kids, and I'd rather not come face to face with a Rain member anymore today.

The clan Coal owns the Wastelands which stretch for a mile beside the school. According to the rules, their job is to collect the garbage and maintain the Wastelands. Despite the disgusting career choice, Coal is the wealthiest clan, which shows in their clothes, their attitude, and the building they live in.

I walk cautiously, flicking wide eyes at every movement and sound. Last night made me jumpy. Being attacked by clan members isn't a regular thing. My biggest threat is Rats like me. They want the black ribbon on my arm, believing if they take it, they'll be safe. And though it might work for a day or two, Tobias would get it back. And whoever had it would be sorry they stole it.

As I approach the Wasteland, Coal members mill about. They wear polo shorts and khakis with Adidas. The girls have makeup and jewelry, watching the boys play a scrimmage game of soccer. Some of them wear a gun at their hip or a knife. They don't pay any attention to me as I go. Tobias and Coal are allies. They may not like me for some reason, but they can't hurt me.

Their building has red brick like the school, but unlike the school, it's beautiful. There is more glass than brick, allowing me to peek inside. A chandelier hangs in the foyer, and black inlaid tile is on the floor. The sound of the air conditioner makes me envious.

Inside the Wastelands, I'm given a bucket and shoved through the gates quickly. There are hills of paper, junk, rotten food, and all else that manifested into the garbage. The bugs are terrible, especially in the middle of summer, and on a hot day like today, they've multiplied. I smack my arms and face, wincing each time I upset a bruise. Pickers, like me, are out searching for any scrap of clothing, items of worth, something that will give them money. I stumble and balance myself over a block of trash before I come to a little private enclave where I can pick up without someone attempting to steal my stuff. I place my bucket down and drop to my knees in the watery bacteria, digging in the muck and shit of a year's worth of foulness. I find little things; a picture frame, a glass jar, and a book bag. I break the glass and get a sizable sharp piece out of it. I find a ripped piece of fabric and wrap it around the glass before sticking it in my pocket. Having a weapon eases so much tension.

An hour in, I take a break. I sit on a broken desk, observing the vast space of trash. Years and years worth. No matter how much they burn it, it never runs out.

Not too far away are the walls. It's a concrete border keeping us locked in here. It's high, like a hundred feet, and taller than our buildings. I've traced the outline of the wall, trying to find a way out, but I gave up when Miss Nancy told us the world out there is more dangerous. I'd rather stay here than journey into an unknown abyss.

What if she lied?

Without a memory of life before this world, I couldn't risk the chance of escaping and having it worse. At least here, I have some kind of protection.

I stuff my bucket with more random crap and hold it close to me. It's minor, but it will get me something good to eat. I don't notice the leg poking out. I trip hard, landing in the softness of the mud. I turn to see, but I catch a sight never seen before.

A pair of shoes.

I frantically look around. There is no one close by, no one to see my discovery. Dead bodies don't usually end up here. They are picked up by Snatchers and taken out.

Who is it? What did they do?

By the expensiveness of their shoes, they had to be from a clan.

Shoes.

I hurry, crawling to the dead person's feet, and grab at the articles, fumbling and gripping. I'm panicking. It's taking too long to get them off; someone else will notice. Tears are in my eyes. I smack the shoes, pull, and yank, beating this person's leg, silently yelling at them to let go, to stop fighting, and to give me the shoes.

I need them now; what good would they serve in the afterlife?

You're dead!

The shoes slip off, and I'm thrown to my butt. I look at them. I don't know what it feels like to wear shoes, but I'm not dumb enough to try them on. I rush, tossing them in my bucket, throwing on the mildew-covered book bag to hide them.

I hesitate. The feet are blue and clean. I look at my own, but they are covered in the black mud I can't tell where I end and it begins. Will death make me clean? So many times, I wondered if it was just better to die. But how will I ever know if it gets better if I did? There is still some part of me dreaming.

I received two hundred tickets. What the hell am I going to do with two hundred tickets? I walk Main street tentatively with my hands in my pocket, clenching the rolls of tickets with tight fists. There are multiple kiosks set up, selling random items. They open before and after school to buy things like clothes, shoes, hair products, makeup, and even bedroom items. I stop in front of kiosk full of clothes. The kid maintaining it is a Coal member and she doesn't take her eyes off me as I rummage to find something I want. A medium gray shirt and sweatpants. They are boy clothes but I'm not picky. I'm pretty sure she up charges me but I have enough to give her. She reluctantly offers me a bag.

Dinner is awesome with a chicken sandwich, strawberries, a chocolate bar, and a nice cup of soda. I've spent this time contemplating my next move. I want to spend the money because I won't be able to hold it forever. Someone's bound to steal it. I've already caught the eye of a Mine member but they glanced at the black ribbon on my arm and thought better of it.

I'm staring at Rain's compound. It's in the back of campus, a four-story building, rectangular in shape. A big spotlight envelopes the entrance. I approach slowly. Rain is supposed to provide shelter, as stated in the rules. I'd love a bath and a bed. But what if I'm walking into the lion's den? Even though Hail protected me at school, is it too much to enter his building? Am I once again pressing my luck?

I guess I'll never know until I find out.

4

Rain

Two guards out front zero in on me. I'm not backing down. I have money, and I'm a customer whether they like me or not.

They lean into each other, whispering, brows knitted in confusion. One of them shrugs before they straighten. "What do you want, Rat?"

I hold up my tickets, "A bath." My weapon gives me a false sense of security, and I clench it tightly.

They glance at each other again. The guard clicks on his walk-talkie, "Hey, Drop...um...we got a customer."

"Yeah, Henry, send them in," a female voice replies.

"It's..." Henry eyes me, "Think you should check them out first."

"Is this a prank again? I'm busy."

Henry sighs and flicks a hand to his partner. The other one approaches and snatches my arm. "We gotta check ya to make sure you ain't carrying anything." He pats my pockets and digs in, pulling out my hand. He rolls his eyes as he yanks away my makeshift shiv.

I keep still. Struggling only makes it worse. Their hands tend to slip to places I don't want to be touched.

The guard pushes me forward, "Cocky dumbass."

Cocky? Is that what I am? If I were cocky, would I possess so much fear?

Inside, my feet are slow. The light illuminates the tile and the rectangular light blue carpet as it leads to the front desk. I walk on the edge of it unwilling to muck it up as my sludge covered flip flops leaves a trail of dirt.

The walls are pristine white with artwork of the ocean. I find myself standing in front of it. The sunsets on one and there is a shadow of a sailboat on the water. Seagulls fly through the air. I can almost hear them call.

"Can I help you?"

I snap my head toward the woman behind the desk.

"Oh," Her smile turns into a reproach and she slowly takes her seat.

I abandon the picture, approaching. The desk is a circle with her comfortably sitting in the middle. There are hallways in every direction but from the left I hear splashing and laughter, a waft of chlorine attacks me. People exit with towels wrapped around them and flip-flops squealing.

The girl behind the desk crosses her arms, leaning back in her computer chair. "Some prank," Drop mutters under her breath before addressing me, "Come to steal more clothes?"

I never have a problem replying with an attitude. I slap the money on the counter, "I want a bath."

She's a beautiful girl. Black hair, black smooth skin, and eyes popping with white eyeshadow. Could I be like her if I lived in a clan? Could I be clean every day and wear fitted clothes? Could my hair be brushed and make-up on point like hers?

She cackles, "Get serious."

"I want a bath," I repeat sternly. Now I'm not leaving without one.

Her finger taps her arm, studying me with a terse mouth. I don't take my eyes away, her stare is nowhere near as intimidating as Tobias'.

"It's a hundred tickets," Drop finally concedes. With a glance at my clothes, she adds, "It's clear you can't afford it."

I slap it on the counter and she eyes the contaminated tickets with a sneer.

"Fine. But if you cause problems, *any more* problems," she stresses. "I'm not saving you."

"Save me? Like you saved me last night? I don't need shit from you. Just a bath."

Footsteps approach lazily against the tile. She snaps her head toward the visitor as he comes around the corner. "Drop, do you have…" Hail's voice fades when he recognizes me. It's awkward, the length of his stare, and then he seems to wake up, "What are you doing here?"

Was there panic in his voice?

Drop replies condescendingly, "She wants a bath."

"Oh," he turns immediately, "Light."

A soldier is at his side. Light's muscles bulge through his blue shirt, short and bulky like a champion fighter. A punch from him would crush me. If he's anything like Cloud, I won't stand a chance against him.

Like Hail, surprise blares on his face when he sees me. His shocking blue eyes shine like a beacon against the darkness of his skin, and I have to pull my gaze away.

"Would you take her to suite five?"

Light stutters, glancing at Hail, to Drop, to me. "Um…Is that a good idea?"

Hail pats his shoulder and leans in to whisper, "Stay outside her door. Don't let anyone in. You understand?"

"Hail..."

"Go on," Hail gestures to me, "It's on us."

Drop tosses a bag on the counter, "This should be fun." She pushes the money back toward me, "Don't piss anyone off."

"I'll try."

I snatch the bag, sticking my head inside it. There's a towel and some toiletries. I leave the money on the counter. I don't want her to think she's doing me any favors.

Light leads the way down the hall. The building is unlike anything I've seen before. Even the Respect House where Tobias stays isn't as extravagant. The hall is silent, our movements the only sound the deeper we get. There are paintings of angels and blue skies that walking in the hall feels like visiting the halls of Heaven. It doesn't seem right that something like this should exist here. Where did they get this stuff? With shipments? I've never seen furniture delivered, only kids.

You think they could spare some time cleaning the locker room, I bitterly sneer.

Light waits at a doorway, looking at me as if he's got something to say. What could a Rain member have to say to me? Does he want to brag about his friends beating the crap out of me last night?

I stop with several feet between us. I don't trust him enough to move.

"You shouldn't be here," Light tells me, looking down the next hall. "Do whatever you have to, but get out soon. I'll be right outside." He opens the door and waits, but after several seconds of us staring at each other, he steps back to give me space. I dart into the room and slap it shut, holding it in place while I look for something to block it. Surprisingly, I notice the lock on the knob, and I tentatively press it and wait. My hand slowly leaves the door.

Cool. It's locked.

It takes another second for it to actually sink in. I turn toward the room. Like the building itself, the room is extravagant: A four-poster bed, a couch, a TV, and separate bathroom.

It's a home.

It's heaven.

Tears well up instantly. I never thought a room like this existed. How can good and nice things be in this world? Why can't I have any of it?

I lean against the large bassinet tub and turn on the faucet. Even though I know water comes from it, I'm amazed to see it running so clean. Clear, warm fresh water is a beautiful sight. My hand dives under it, the pressure like a tropical storm. Around it are oils, lotions, bubbles, lavenders, and vanilla-scented bath bombs. I'm smelling everything, wondering if I can keep any of it.

The heat of the water sends vapor into the air. I can't wait to sink into it, but my apprehension hasn't faded. The man outside the door keeps me on edge. I know enough locks aren't break-proof.

I told myself not to look at my body, but I couldn't help it. I stand in front of a mirror. Bruises circle both my thighs. Black, blue, purple, and all colors in between. The welt on my ribs looks bigger. Scratch marks trail down my lower back and bottom, where the boys dragged me for fun.

My knees hit the floor in front of the toilet, where I throw up everything inside of me. It hurts so bad, but I empty my stomach until my body is satisfied. I lean back against the wall wiping my mouth on my clothes. I glare at the door as if daring Light to come in.

What's he thinking?

When the tub is full, I put only a foot in, squeamish from the heat. I watch the mud mix with the water. I hate how just a single appendage destroys the clear liquid.

Angered, I throw the rest of my body in, squealing. The water quickly blackens from my filthy parts. I drain it while I fill it up, using the flowing water as a hose for the worst spots. I wash, scrub and scratch, removing all the grime I possibly can. Wounds reopen, and blood awakens, which only irritates me.

It takes time, but now I'm satisfied. I shut off the water, and it's actually transparent. I smile in accomplishment.

The water always clears.

I lean back, resting my head against the tub. My eyes land on the door.

What does he think of me?

A prideful rat?

Tobias' girlfriend?

From a distance, I can see the black ribbon on the floor.

'Wear it,' Tobias said. 'To let everyone know you belong to me.'

From the first day, Tobias has controlled everything I do. I could stay with him, live in his building, and be an actual member of Respect, but it would mean giving him parts of me I don't want to share.

In consequence, he forbade the clans from letting me in.

"Yo Light, the boys and I've been looking for you." I hear

a voice right outside my door. It's a familiar sound, one that freezes me where I am.

"Hey, Cloud, I'm stuck with house duty tonight."

I sit up, wrapping my arms around my chest, scrunching up into a tight ball. The water splashes, and there is quiet behind the door.

"New recruit?"

"Customer," Light replies carelessly.

"You know, I heard a funny little rumor." His voice explodes, "That Tobias' BITCH had the nerve to come into this house!"

I stand up, "Who are you calling a bitch?" Dripping wet and naked probably isn't the best way to start a fight. I flip my eyes madly about searching for a weapon. I could break off a leg of a chair. I make a move, but sounds from outside the door stop me.

Scuffling, and maybe a punch? "Enough," Light demands.

"You serious, bro?"

"Are *you* serious? You beat up a girl? What the hell, man?"

"That's not a girl. It's Tobias' slut. And I did what everyone else was afraid to do."

"I don't get you. I should turn you in. Just get out of here. If Drop or Hail learns it was you, they're gonna kick you out."

"Drop won't do shit besides talk my ear off." He pounds on the door, making me jump, "You got some fucking balls coming here. Think you're safe, huh?"

Safe. I'm not safe anywhere.

"Back off!" Light growls, and after an odd thumping sound against the door, there is a second of silence.

Cloud calms when he speaks, "Tobias killed Shock three days ago. Our best friend. The fucker gets away with it because he's in with the Teachers. It's bullshit. I got revenge like the clan creed. 'An eye for an eye.' I didn't do anything wrong."

"Shock hit a teacher, Cloud. Tobias had no choice. And that girl has nothing to do with it."

"No choice? How could you stick up for him? You know, people are talking about you joining that stupid rebellion. You don't believe it, do you? That little bitch in there is not going to save anyone."

If he calls me a bitch one more time, I'm gonna drown him in the tub.

"Times are changing, Cloud. If you want to stay in this clan, I'd change with it. If you don't like it, take it up with Hail."

The name drops, and a switch is flipped. More silence follows, and even I can feel the tension through the door. Cloud seems to give up. "I get it. Don't get all upset. Don't go tell *daddy* on me."

There are things about this place I don't understand. If I could get into a clan, I might get some bearing, learn about it and figure out where I belong. I could have a friend.

Tobias would never allow it.

What I do know is I have been protected for the first time, and it makes me wonder if it is some sort of ruse. Why protect me if not for his own personal gain? But what do I have to give?

A soft knock on the door, "Sorry. He's gone. I'll be out here until you're done. You're safe."

It's the single most important word blinking in my head. *Safe. Safe. Safe.*

My lips tighten, and my throat clenches. Tears are already rolling down my cheeks. I force out a whisper, "Thank you."

It's silent as I stare at the door.

"You're welcome."

5

Not Her

I slip on my sweatpants and a gray shirt, taking heed of my damaged ribs. I flick my wet hair out and notice my reflection in the mirror. I don't cringe. I'm proud for a moment. These clothes weren't stolen nor covered in blood. They aren't given to me by Tobias because he wants me in *something pretty.* I earned them with my hours spent in the Wasteland. And whoever shoes I found.

Was it Shock? Would a clan member end up in the Wastelands?

I brush my hair, winching from a dozen knots. I would love to cut it all off and have it end at my chin or shoulders. It rides far down my back, a matted mess, and the sweat on my neck from the heat worsens it. But I'm not allowed to cut it.

Or I could do it anyway and take the consequences.

Some punishments are worth it. Stealing from Rain after they beat me was worth it. But upsetting Tobias is different. I never want to push him too far. There are threats of things he could still do to me, and I don't want to find them out.

My fingers play with the rough edges of it as I stare back at my reflection. With my cheeks red from the bath heat, my blue eyes are bright and clear. Around them are dark circles caused by sleepless nights. I move in close to look at my cheeks, slightly sunken by my low appetite. It's not like food isn't plentiful here. Even if I couldn't afford it, I could still get it. I simply need to ask for help. It sounds easy, but my pride won't allow it. I don't want anyone to do anything for me. Better yet, I don't want to owe anyone anything. Tobias taught me what it means to owe, and I'm still reaping those *benefits* every time he comes near me.

Determination sets fire to my heart. I feel strong here. I feel as if I know who I am for a brief moment. I'm indestructible.

Happiness wiggles through me. I run to the bed, jumping on it like a little kid finding a stale piece of bread. I grasp my pillow, hugging it, taking in the fresh scent of washed linens. It is all too beautiful, too perfect. I wrap the red blankets around me and curl into a small ball, ready to fall into an ever-blissful sleep.

My thoughts run rampant, my eyes refusing to shut. I want to give into a rejuvenating rest, but I am still scared. I stare at the door, at Light. Can he feel it? He probably hates it. He hates me, I'm sure, for making him work when his friends want him to hang out. I am nothing. I'm an obligation; I don't even come up on his radar as something to get upset about.

A knock shoots me to my feet.

"Sorry to interrupt. It's Drop."

I move along the wall, searching for a weapon to give me leverage. I grab a hairbrush.

"Can we talk?"

What could she possibly have to say to me?

I hold my 'weapon' before me, tiptoeing to the door. With a quick click of the lock, I shoot back to the opposite side of the room.

Drop opens the door. Her beauty is like a cactus flower. Sweet but with hidden thorns. She smiles, and her eyes sparkle like stars. Light is behind her, staring at me from over her shoulder.

She holds up a plastic bag, "I brought you some undergarments. I assume you don't have any."

Drop is oddly nicer than she was hours ago. I don't like it.

"I don't take charity."

She shifts unsteadily, "It's part of the umm…service, I just didn't have any to give you."

She tosses it toward me, but I don't move, keeping the brush out in front of me.

"I wanted to apologize," she pauses, attempting to shove down her pride, "For my attitude earlier. I had just finished listening to complaints about you."

"They left their stuff," I fight lamely.

Drop ignores me. She obviously doesn't want to be here; her eyes keep shifting toward the door. "I didn't approve of what happened last night."

She says it carelessly like they stole a hair tie from me.

"If you give me a name, I'll see them punished."

"Oh, you'll send them to their room?"

She laughs bitterly as if I'm the one being ridiculous when she shouldn't even be here. "Rain and Respect aren't in a good place. I'm trying to fix it, and I'd appreciate a little help."

"Help?" It's my turn to laugh. "From me? What can a little Rat do for a clan member?"

Drop rolls her eyes, "You really are something." She leans in, whispering, "I know you're lying. You convinced everyone you're here to save us, but I'm not dumb. I knew Memory."

"Who the hell is Memory?"

Drop is silent, debating if it's another lie. She's angry at me for something, but all I've done is try to survive.

She shakes her head, mumbling, "I keep saying you aren't her, and no one believes me." Drop turns out of the room, "You guys are wrong," she murmurs to Light.

"Please, Drop."

"You want a savior so badly you ignore the facts. She isn't her." Drop yanks the door closed.

I'm alone, holding a hair brush. I toss it on the dresser, cursing my existence. What would I have done with a stupid hairbrush? "Very intimidating."

I struggle with sleep, lying under the bed with blankets all around me. I've never felt safe or as comfortable, but Drop's words kept repeating in my head.

'She isn't her.' Who have they mistaken me for? Is that why Tobias won't leave me alone? He thinks I'm someone I'm not? Or maybe I am her, and I've forgotten. I would love to be someone important. It would make all this worth it.

Too soon, the bed is shaking. "Hey. Girl. It's time."

My eyes snap open, my heart pounding, my body reacting with instinct, squeezing myself as tight and small as I could be, pressing against the wall begging to be invisible. Quick questions raid my mind.

Where is my weapon? Where am I? What section of the world am I in? How far am I away from the Cafe?

I could only see his dark blue shoes before the teen drops to his knee. Light's blue eyes catch mine. A sigh escapes his lips, "Come on, girl. I'm not going to hurt you."

Light peers behind him, a glance of purpose, before he looks back at me, "Get out of here. This is not a safe place for you right now." He abandons the room, leaving me with his cryptic message, a message from my savior.

Taking his warning, I leave the room behind with only the clothes on my back. I search for Light, ridiculously hoping to see him one last time. He's too good-looking for this place. It's annoying.

Upon the exit, two guards remain. They watch me, different kids from earlier, and their eyes widen when they realize who I am.

My attention spans the campus I've come to know as the world. Dirt roads, mildew covered buildings, no trees and the sun burns the ground. It's hideous, another version of hell. I turn back to the Rain building. It's a beautiful rose in a land of cacti. I don't want to leave it. Even with Light's warning, I want to stay here. All the work I put into myself, fixing, cleaning, and mending, will be gone by tomorrow.

"She's gonna beg," one guard says to another.

"She might not."

"They all beg."

A chuckle, "Yeah. They do."

It's at that moment my weakness leaves me.

I know what I have to do.

I run.

6

Charles

Leaving the Rain compound, I don't need to look back when I hear the trampling feet behind me. Mine members are always watching, scouting for fresh meat. They think I have something worth stealing. Leaving Rain means I had tickets, and they want to ensure I have nothing left.

I can take three routes: down the center of Open Alley and straight into the cafe. If I'm lucky, they hadn't thought to put helpers there to block my entrance. If I turn right, around the back of the school, turn left and go up Black Alley, throw myself through the third window on the right, or go down Dark Alley and end up in the Respect building. Black Alley and Dark Alley are on opposite sides of the school, the apartments are too close together, so it's parts of the road that never see the light of day.

I take a right since the left is already cut off by three more Mine members. They run like lizards, with fast little feet on short legs.

School starts in two hours. The sky is beginning to lighten. I have to find somewhere to hide until then. I have to figure out how to get to the cafe to have some breakfast.

I'm running faster than their little legs can catch. A smile is on my lips even as I'm huffing for air. Despite running out of fear, I still love running. It's become a game to see who is faster.

It's always me.

Boundary Members watch us with humor, unwilling to intercept. I really don't understand the reason for their existence. They have no interest in helping, yet their job is to keep the peace.

Right before I turn down Black Alley to hide, a gunshot sounds, scaring me enough to keep going straight around the Rats' building. Out of disorientation, once the building on my right ends, I dodge behind it, going further down only to meet a dead end.

I swing to the left, where there is a small enclave to fit a fire escape, and hide beneath it. My chest heaves as I press my back against the wall. I hear footsteps in the sand, and I suck in my last breath to stop making a sound.

"You lost her," one little kid pouts.

"I didn't lose her; you lost her."

I look around my environment. I'm completely hidden back here. Above me is a fire escape fifteen feet up with no ladder. And though I'm trapped, I realize something.

I could live back here.

"It's because of this slow-ass newbie."

I peek around the bend. It's dark here, and I'm hidden in the shadows. I can see three boys at the alley's entrance. They are small, no older than ten, with shaved heads, and they dress in rags and bare feet.

"I don't think she came down here," the smallest one whimpers.

"We know you're here!" the tallest kid shouts, "Come on out, and we won't knife ya. New Kid, go get her."

The little black kid shrinks, "I..I don't... I don't know what to do."

"Now's a good time to learn. It's just a girl. If you fail, we'll kill ya."

"I..I don't want to," he whispers.

The two boys don't waste one moment before they start punching him. The child falls to the ground, curling into a tight ball, crying out as they kick him, taking turns to stomp on his ribs and knees.

My breath comes heavy as I watch the assault. If I help, the Mine Members will only come after me. I don't go looking for fights. I have enough to deal with on my own, and it's not like they will kill the newbie.

The little kid needs to toughen up anyway.

But his screams echo in my ears. They remind me of my own.

Cursing myself, I run as fast as possible, and with my arms out, I bulldoze right into two of them, knocking them to the ground. I get to my feet first and watch as they rise. The left one whips out a knife and runs at me. I slap his hand, shoving my fist into his throat, and he falls to the floor in a choking fit. I have sand in my other hand and throw it in the face of the second assailant. I dart down for the knife the boy dropped.

I look at the little kid curled on the floor, "Hey, get up. We have to run."

As the left boy clears the sand out of his face and the other begins to catch his breath again, I get nervous. At any moment, more members of Mine can come to their aid, and my battle will be lost. Mine are like cockroaches. They are everywhere; they come from every nook and cranny.

If the boys paid any attention, they would note I'm good with both hands, but considering they aren't good at fighting, I'm going to act like I haven't shown my secret. I wave the knife, keeping their attention where I want as I get closer and closer until one of them dives for the blade, and I shove the palm of my free hand into his face, breaking his nose. He falls with a cry and squirting blood.

The other isn't stupid. He even smiles at me. "You must be that freak Rat I heard about. The rumors about you aren't wrong, I guess. But you're still just a girl." I swing the blade again, but he isn't paying attention. Perhaps he doesn't think I'll use it. He's right, but that doesn't mean I don't have tricks up my sleeve.

I tuck the knife into my pants and put my fists up. He laughs but concedes getting into a fighting position. He moves in to punch me, making the correct judgment I would hit him with my right. I throw my hand back, punch, and miss. He goes in to grip my arm, and without realizing it, I punch him in the face with my left. He falls to the floor, and I jump over him, pressing the blade to his neck.

"Get out of here," I demand.

I wait for his fearful nod and hop off. They pick each other up, embarrassed more than anything.

"We're gonna come back for you!" he hollers as he darts away.

"Do it!" I scream, "I'll break your nose too."

My attention returns to the little kid, having turned my

back. I curse at myself, knowing how disastrous that could have been. But my instincts work fine because the child is still on the ground shaking and sniveling.

I don't like hurting people, but I've spent three months here, I needed to learn how to protect myself. I would have never survived otherwise. This pathetic kid isn't going to last a week.

I ought to go, I know. I look at the spot I found, the secret hole that could be my salvation. There are Coal guards at the Coal entrance, twenty feet away and they eye us out of bored interest. I wish I had something to hide my face. I don't like being in the spotlight. The fewer people who know my face, the safer I feel. Yet, as that kid mentioned, I've already made a name for myself.

Freak Rat isn't much better than Scream.

I look at the kid, still crying and ignorant of what's happening. I notice the band on his wrist.

A Newbie.

I tuck the knife into my waistband. Catching sight of my clean hands, I make the grand realization of my obligation.

I dig my fingers into the dirt. I rub it into my fresh linens, picking up more and smashing it into my pants. My mouth hardens, ripping the hem of my shirt, pulling at the collar till it falls over my naked shoulder. I press soil into my beautifully brushed hair, clumping it, knotting it, till the fresh smell is a lingering scent in my memory. Lastly, I massage my face with dust over my chapped lips and healing cheeks.

I am normal again. Somehow, I feel protected.

The kid continues to whimper on the ground. But he isn't my concern.

I take a step away.

If you leave him, you are only proving the teachers right.

With an annoyed sigh, I kneel down beside him. He flinches when I reach for him. "Hey. Stop that," I chide. "You got to be a man now."

"I just turned nine," he whimpers.

My heart fastens.

How does he know?

I look over my shoulder, scared Tobias is testing me. Questions aren't allowed, yet they tease my lips, about to escape.

My eagerness must have caught his attention. He looks up with light green eyes, surrounded by black and blue bruises. A broken lip, a swollen nose. His bald scalp had dried blood in places that were nicked. "I had my birthday last week. I got a bike."

"You..." I swallow, licking my lips, dying from the thirst for information. "You remember?"

"Yeah, it just happened." He rubs the snot from his nose with the back of his hand as he sits up. "I shouldn't have run away." He wraps his arms around his knees, burying his face, "I want my mommy."

I pull at his arm, and he gets up, limping, stumbling as I push him. I lead him to a Rat building and sit down on a stairway.

I need answers before someone takes him away.

"You came with the last shipment on Saturday?"

He nods.

When shipments come, it's presented like a great event. Everyone gathers at the entrance, watching those big cement doors open, hoping to catch a view outside the white walls. After the first month, the excitement had dwindled for me. Behind those doors was a whole other set of barriers.

Shipments are delivered on a school bus. A man name Prod greets them, making them scamper out the back to escape his electric prod stick. Then the clans attack.

"Do you..."

I'm scared to ask. I'm afraid he'll disappear like everyone that's ever talked to me. "Do you remember out there?"

"Yeah. Don't you?"

I shake my head, staring at him like he's an angel. "What's out there?"

He shrugs, "Home."

Home? Do I have a home?

"I'm Charles. What's your name?"

It is a question I've never heard before. It never mattered to me what anyone called me. A name is just a name, and it's not who I am, nor who I'm meant to be. Looking down at this little boy, I am ashamed I haven't gotten a better name to give.

"My name is Scream."

He scrunches up his face. "Really? That's weird."

My defensiveness is quicker than the speed of light, "Charles is stupid," I snap.

"No, it's not!"

The tears he cried are already drying. I am amazed at how quickly he heals. I wish I could be like that.

7

Alone

H*ome.*
I stare at the walls now as if I could see through them.

"There's nothing out there for you." Tobias kicked me in my stomach, *"Your parents are dead. You have no family. I'm your family."*

I believed him because he was all I knew. I was empty when I arrived here, and Tobias filled me with poison. What was true and what wasn't? How can I ever spot the difference?

Is my home out there? I never looked hard enough for an exit, and I was afraid to actually find one. Miss Nancy shows us in every class the existence of murderers. The amount of death that exists is far more significant than here. We may be bad kids, but death is forbidden. Logically, this place is safer.

And I wouldn't have Tobias' protection outside the walls.

"So what is this place?"

I look at Charles, having forgotten he was there. I don't have the time to teach him. I've got to work on escape.

I fill Charles in on the basics for survival. Wait for Saturday, join the Harvest, and get in a clan.

I abandoned him at that point. I don't need this kid to think I can possibly help him. But he follows me.

I yell at him to go away, throw a few rocks, and quicken my pace to a sudden sprint. He's surprisingly clingy, but I need to get him gone.

Tobias won't like it, and what he didn't like, he'd take away.

My stomach rumbles. I could go for a big breakfast, and with the tickets still in my pocket, I could afford the good stuff. I glance over my shoulder. Charles' big bright green eyes watch me unsure, but his body is tense, ready to follow or run depending on my mood. My hand feels the money in my pocket. I guess sharing won't be so terrible.

I slow my pace. It takes him no time to catch up.

We walk into Main street. The morning was already getting hot with the summer heat, but it didn't stop kids from setting up their kiosks. It's primarily full of clan members, each color sticking to its own. A few glances make me uneasy, and I keep checking to ensure my ribbon doesn't fall off. I would love to buy a pair of shorts and a tank top so I'm not sweating, but I can't risk revealing too much skin.

Charles gets scared quickly. There are dozens of kids, and though it's not a perilous time, it's intimidating as Boundary members walk around with rifles hanging off their shoulders. Charles sometimes comes up close, grabbing my fingers, and I keep yanking them from him. He needs to toughen up fast.

The cafeteria is on the first floor of a Rat building. The whole first floor of the building is open, with the metal doors bunched into a corner. Rat buildings don't have air conditioning, so big fans hang on the ceiling providing a breeze. It is usually crowded for breakfast. Rows of benches and tables stretch out, constantly patrolled by Boundary members to keep the peace.

"This is a safe zone; violence is illegal. If you get in trouble, come here."

I get in line. The problem with the cafeteria is the food sucks. It's basic mush and the same old stuff every day. If you want variety, you have to pay for it. My money goes towards chocolate. I'm good with sharing my money, but he better not reach for a piece of my candy.

"Why am I here? Why are we all here?"

"You think I know?" I bite.

Attitude much?

I chastise myself for being mean. I'm not used to talking to people who aren't being jerks to me. But he annoys me.

Why?

He's a child, stupid and weak, and he doesn't understand what this place is. He's lucky.

I'm jealous?

I scoff, laughing. He eyes me suspiciously, but I don't pay attention. Jealous, what a ridiculous thing. We're in the same predicament now. I push out the badness in my stance and release the frown on my lips. The boy has enough trouble; he doesn't need a bratty girl getting snotty with him for no reason.

"Scream."

I smile in greeting, "Hey, Zack."

Zack holds out his thin arms, his bracelets jingling. He has an open shirt of flowers and short pants that reach mid-thigh, and beachy flip-flops, ready for vacation in this hellhole.

I embrace him lightly, glancing at the two guards following him. I pull back, bowing my head. Zack gives me a bad feeling in the pit of my stomach, but he's been nice to me since I've come here, so I try to suppress it as much as I can. He touches my face with his bejeweled fingers.

Despite being considered a teacher, Zack describes himself as the 'loveable uncle'. He is the only teacher who stays on campus. Zack is the ruler of Spread, a clan devoted to love. He owns the cafe, and right across the street is Spread's main house with billowing curtains hanging from the doorframe.

"I searched for you the other day. I heard Rain was going to lash out at Respect."

I glance back at Charles, who stands there, giving Zack an odd stare. "What does that have to do with me?" I whisper, winching when he puts some cream on my cuts. I wish he wouldn't baby me in front of everyone; I can feel their disgusted stares.

"Everyone knows Tobias loves you, darling. He's a big old grumpy bear with the heart of a kitten." Zack giggles, brushing my hair back. I yank away from him, hating his grooming. He lifts a hand in surrender and slips the ointment into his pocket. "Tough bug, you are. I need someone like you in my clan." Over his shoulder, I observe the faces of his two guards. Stoic and machine-like, they barely blink as they stand there.

"Who is this?" Zack wonders and reaches a hand out to touch Charles' face.

I step in front of him, pulling Charles behind me, "My friend."

Zack takes a step back, "Oh. How nice you finally have a friend." He looks down at the boy one more time before stepping around me. "Spread the Love!" he waves, reciting his clan's slogan. His guards follow, and I keep still till they have passed.

"Who was that?" Charles asks. "I don't like him."

I observe the guards. They wear all white, even down to their shoes. Their hair is oiled and slicked back, not a piece out of place. There is no emotion, no human quality to them. And they are older, no longer little kids but nearly adults. To have such control over a person, I can't imagine what they've been through.

I'd rather be friends with Zack than be an enemy. It's all about survival. His building is right next to Tobias'. If I ever needed an escape, Zack would take me in. Zack is the only clan leader who isn't afraid of Tobias. But I will keep my guard up around him.

I pile my plate full of eggs, toast, bacon, and strawberries for dessert. Food is thankfully cheap when I actually have tickets. Charles digs in like I knew he would. I pack some bacon away for later in the day. Six hours of straight school is hard enough without being hungry.

Charles asks a billion questions. I answer only the ones I'm sure of, but they aren't very descriptive, and he gets frustrated in a flash. It is funny how quickly he gets riled up, and I found myself poking fun for the sport of it.

We walk toward the brick building of the school, and Charles curses. "I still have to go to school? What crap!"

"Don't miss." I point to the cameras in every corner of the world. "They will send someone for you."

"Who's 'they'?"

I shrug.

'They' are the people making the rules, but I don't know exactly who they are.

"First month, first floor. Every day, the class changes. It's like bingo. Whatever the teachers want to teach that day. Sometimes it will be interesting, but most of the time, it's boring."

"So normal school," he sighs.

I suppress a smile.

There's school out there. What else could there be?

I bring him to his first class, overloaded with new students who don't know where to go. I wish him luck and separate hastily to journey to my own class before the bell rings.

"Wait," he calls, hurrying after with his short legs. I pretend not to hear him. "Wait, please!"

My feet stop on their own.

I swing at him, pushing my temper out. "Look, kid, join a clan. Don't be a Rat. That's the best thing for you." I snap around, hoping he'll give up any further protest. The first week is always the worst, but the moment he joins a clan, it will improve, and he will be fine without me. Probably even more so.

I lose his voice in the crowd.

I scold myself when I look back for him, but I'm not surprised when I can't find him. It is better this way. Rats are alone for a reason.

I am alone for a reason.

8

Tobias

My class is on the third floor for my third month. I like classrooms with a window despite the bars they have. It's brighter and allows me to daydream. I peek into one to see if there are any seats left. But because I am a little late, most spots are taken, and I go down the hall to the next room.

There is an empty chair in the last class, and I rush to it before the bell rings.

The familiar whispers are directed at my back. I hear the name 'Memory' again, and I swing around if only to tell them I have no idea who that is, but words catch in my throat when I see my guard from Rain, Light.

I don't usually pay attention to faces; it's hard to do when my head is always down. He feels my gaze and flicks his blue eyes toward me. He squeezes his lips in acknowledgment, then focuses on his surrounding friends.

I straighten, leaning into my desk in a chance to appear smaller than I am. My eyes flick to the corner, pathetically trying to catch sight of him again. It's stupid what I feel, even if I don't know what it is exactly. Maybe it's because he's cute that I can't get him out of my thoughts. Or maybe because he protected me from Cloud, his own clanmate, that confuses me.

A hand drops on my desk. Clean and trimmed fingernails with intricate tattoos weaving on every finger and a four-letter word engraved on the knuckles: FEAR.

My breath comes heavy as a wave of panic, terror, and rage swirls in my chest. Tobias stands at my desk, waiting for my attention. I struggle with swallowing the disgust building in my throat. Terrible thoughts begin to form. I don't hurt people. I never want bad things to happen to them. But Tobias makes the demon in me come out. The devil is what this place says I have in me. It's why I'm here. I can't help but think they're right when I'm around him. Why else would I have such heinous fantasies?

I know better than to ignore him. I lean back, and let him see my face. I hope he notices loathing. I hope he could see how I'd run a blade through his chest if I had the chance. I'd follow the path of the scar on his face, only I'd press harder.

Tobias admires me with affection in his dirty brown eyes. His thin lips curve into a smirk, broken by the scar running up his face. I envy that scar. I wish I had been the one to give it to him. I like how it ruins whatever good looks he would have had. I hope it hurt when it happened. I hope he cried.

Tobias raises his gaze toward the Rain members in the back. His jaw clenches, the muscles in his cheeks flexing.

"Tobias," I greet him only to stop whatever trouble he might cause.

Tobias' attention falls back on me. He smiles, "Scream." He

lifts his hand and tucks my ill-begotten hair from my face. I close my eyes at his touch, cringing, the smell of nicotine drenching him.

"Listen to me," he whispered in my ear, *"I'll protect you. But first, I'm gonna make you scream."*

My body shivers.

Tobias rests a finger under my chin, "Stay after class. I want to spend some time with you today." He kisses my forehead, "You can sit in the back with me," he offers, but he doesn't force and leaves me where I am.

I exhale with relief.

I can hear him. Every move he makes causes an unconscious shudder. His laugh is like a squeaking staircase. His friends rally around him as if he is something worth speaking to. But they do it out of fear, just like I do.

I watch him through the tendrils of my long hair. My curiosity is piqued by confusion. How can a person be so contradicting? Looking at him now, he seems normal. A teenage kid, laughing, fun, easy going, perfect to any outsider.

My only answer is a confirmed fact. Tobias is what Miss Nancy talks about. The evil that exists in him, he releases proudly and without shame.

I glance in Light's direction. He's on the opposite side of the room with his clan mates around him. He glares vehemently at Tobias. There is a devil in him too. He was pretending to care about me because it was his job. I need to get that into my head before I make any ignorant mistakes.

When class is over, I think about running. I could dive out before Tobias has a chance to get me. But if I ran, he would find me later, proving to be a most painful warning. The children empty the room. I get up from my chair, and Tobias leans against the wall by the exit. He grabs my arm right at the last moment and pulls me in front of him, chuckling, finding my unwillingness humorous.

His thumb touches the bruises on my arm, "I'm sorry you got caught up in this, baby. I'm fixing it. It would help me a bit if you didn't steal clothes from clan members." He smirks fondly, kissing my temple. "You like getting in trouble, don't you? So I can come to your rescue?"

I pull away, I try to, but he has a firm grip on my arm. He takes my hand in his, playing with my fingers like we are sweethearts in love. I swallow, trying not to rip my hand out of his. I don't want to be hit. I don't want to wake his temper, but how do I keep my pride in the process?

"You know they went after you to get to me."

"Should I be honored?" I bite, keeping my head turned away.

He doesn't like that, and his grip on my arm tightens enough to make me wince.

I dare him. Back me into a corner and I will stick my knife in his gut with no remorse.

"You'd be safe beside me, Scream. No one would ever touch you."

"Except you."

"Is that so bad? Being protected and having a home?"

Home. There is no home here. Only out there.

"Yes."

The muscles in his jaw clench, "You know it's me that keeps you alive. That keeps you from the Auction."

Kids stand in the hallway feet from us, looking over their shoulders, watching. No one stops him. No one saves me.

Would Memory save me?

"Who is Memory?"

Tobias straightens, rigid as he stands in front of me now. "What did I tell you about asking questions?"

I bow my head. His tone is a warning, and though I want to fight him, I'm still in pain from yesterday. "Don't."

"Don't," he repeats.

But it's important. I can feel it. Something inside of me needs to know, "But, that boy yesterday said Memory was coming."

Tobias cups my face. I grip his wrists, trying to pull him away, but he's stronger. "Do you remember anything?" The desperation in his face stalls my fear, and I observe him with confusion.

What does he think I should know?

"No."

All the emotion drains on his face, out of his body, and he sags against the wall. I don't move, hoping he'll give me something to understand.

"I want you to stay in the house."

I sneer, "No."

"Rain is trying me. You think it won't get worse? I can't always stop what happens to you."

"What have you stopped?" I bitterly ask.

Tobias scoffs with a smile, "I wonder if you were this dumb before you forgot everything."

I step away, but he grabs my arm, yanking me to him. He kisses me even as I struggle. Panic hits me like a lightning strike, and I trip over myself in desperate need to escape.

Tobias cackles as he moves for the door. "Don't do anything stupid, as hard as that may seem."

I grab the knife from my belt and pace the empty schoolroom. Just holding the weapon makes me feel stronger and in more control. If he comes back, I will attack with everything I have. He makes me feel dumb, like I can't do anything right. I hate how I can't remember. Am I the only one with no memories of the world? What's wrong with me?

A mirror is before me at the back of the classroom, and I catch sight of my face. Would Tobias still want me if I wasn't so damned' beautiful' as he says I am? If I became ugly and horribly deformed, would he leave me alone?

I lift the blade, the tip resting upon my cheek, and I press it hard, so hard blood soaks the entrance before sliding down my chin and mixing with a stray tear.

"That won't help."

I see her in the corner of the mirror. "Now you?"

Tara represents everything I hate. She is everything I will never allow myself to be.

Tara is the only female in Respect. Her black hair is braided with pink and purple strands. She wears a white blouse and a black skirt. She has pretty makeup on her eyes, pink and purple like her hair.

No matter what she wears or how well she takes care of herself, she still makes me sick.

"You've been here, what? Two, three months now?"

"Three."

The shortest eternity I've ever known.

"And you're just now thinking of this?" she snorts. "Come on. Tobias will get mad if you do that."

"What do I care?"

"You should, you know. He goes out of his way to keep you safe."

"Where was he two days ago when Rain came after me?"

"Listen, girl. Here's some advice. Drop this crusade. You're no different from us. You are us." She laughs as those horrid words leave her lips.

I'm not bad. I'm not evil.

"When you finally come around, you'll find there are some pretty good things to this life."

I face her, my knife pointing its red tip in her direction. Her smirk doesn't fail. "There is nothing here that's *good*. This is a sick place that will be destroyed one day."

"By who? You?" she giggles. "Oh, child, it's time to grow up, darling." She sways out of the room, her heels clicking against the tile until I can hear them no more. My knees weaken, and I fall with a hard thump to the ground. My hands catch me, my knife slamming against the floor.

I huff like a spoiled child, too angry to cry and too scared to scream. I want to run, knock down all the walls in my way and go. The fact there is nothing I can do only quickens the pour of cement over my desecrated body.

Footsteps slap against the marble, and I snap my head up, ready to holler at Tara or Tobias or whoever disrupts me. My fumes fizzle in defeat when I find Charles' puffy red eyes. He limps, babying his left leg, which is now swollen and red.

I straighten myself. My self-pity runs dry as I look at him. He has come for reassurance, for strength, and he has come to me. How can I be weak in front of him? Charles needs me.

Someone actually needs me.

I force a smile, "How was school?"

9

Selfish

I scout our previous hideout. How I ended up over in this section of the campus is a mystery, but it seems too perfect. The alley is right in between Coal's two buildings. There is a small section for the emergency escape route in the back. It is empty and roomy enough for an ideal home.

There is only one problem. There are soldiers.

They are unconcerned about the little hideaway I have my eye on. It is unreachable, really. To get to it, we will pass by two Coal soldiers with .38 caliber pistols, and there is always the constantly surveying team of Boundary.

I notice a certain quality, however. During their surveillance, Boundary doesn't go down the alley, and the Coal members are more interested in talking to each other than paying attention to what's behind them.

It will take flawless timing to get there, and I must watch closely, but I'm constantly looking over my shoulder. Where I sit is a dangerous waiting place. This is a Rat-infested building. Mine factions and bored clan members like to play in these structures. I use the word 'play' loosely. Beating kids up and using us as target practice for their malicious paintball games are typical occurrences.

Charles and I stay by the window. I mark each soldier, taking in their positions, attention spans, and lack of care. I am sure no one ever tried to get into this place, which is perfect for us.

Charles isn't a patient child. He sits beside me, picking at his scabs, and asking questions I don't know how to answer.

"You have brothers or sisters?"

I shrug. It amazes me how much Charles knows.

"What are you from? I'm from Texas."

I roll my eyes.

"What's your favorite video game? I love Minecraft."

I've never heard of Minecraft.

"Who do you think would do this to us? Does the government know? My dad says the government knows everything," he stalls and looks out. I thought he saw something, but his gaze is distant. "I was mad at my dad, so I left."

I scoff. "Forget it. It doesn't matter." My response is harsh because of jealousy. I can't remember anything; why does he have all his memories?

"I didn't say goodbye."

"Shut it and pay attention."

He sends a glare my way. "What are we looking at anyway?" he crawls up beside me and leans out the window.

"A hiding place."

"Can't we just go?"

"We have to wait."

"Why?"

"Because I don't want to die."

"Is there anything here to do for fun?"

How can he not understand? Doesn't he get it? His light green eyes are wide and fearless. He's utterly clueless about everything around him. He doesn't see things the way I see them. It is like he is in his own little world.

How do I get there?

I'm thankful when he falls asleep. His head is on my lap. His bald scalp is pricking my hand, yet I can't help running my fingers upon it. It's weird being around this kid. I feel more confident, like I'm stronger, and I know it's wrong. I know I'm no stronger than I was yesterday. But I could put up a commendable fight.

For him.

How long will I be able to keep him? I've never had a friend in this place.

I thought at first it was me that scared people away, but then I realized it was Tobias. No one wanted to risk befriending me. And the ones that tried, I never saw again.

How long until Tobias takes Charles?

I rest my head back, my eyes going to the window, catching sight of the distant stars. As awkward as it may be, this is the most content I have been. It's ridiculous to be comfortable in hell.

I straighten my gaze to the damaged room. The wood floor is cracked and broken. The wallpaper is shredded and moldy and decorated with splashes of paint. Another person curls in the corner, wrapped in a nice blanket. What I would do for that blanket. I have a knife. Perhaps I should steal it for Charles. I pull the weapon out, my heart racing as adrenaline rushes through my veins.

I squeeze my eyes shut in disgust. I'm so awful. I can't let this world get to me. I have to stay good. No matter how hard it becomes. But how? What if I can't? What if one day I have to hurt someone to save myself? Or to save Charles?

I should get rid of him. He's not imperative to my survival. If anything else, he's a weakness I can't afford. He'll slow me down. He'll get me noticed when all I want is to be invisible. But I don't want to be alone anymore. I don't want to struggle by myself.

Shit, I'm so selfish.

I cut his wristband. Now no clan will claim him. He will be mine. My partner and my friend. I condemn him to a life as a Rat. Tears drip down my cheeks because of the self-hatred spurring inside.

Charles moves, and I stiffen. His fingers wrap around the hem of my shirt, pulling it tighter to him. My fingers stroke his peach fuzz. I even find myself humming a song I don't know to help lure him back to sleep.

10

Rule Thirteen

I wake frantically when Charles moves. My eyes wide in panic, I take in my surroundings, my weapon, my escape route. These questions are natural in my process, but I am forming one more: Where is Charles?

He sits beside me with a weird face. "Do you always wake up like that?"

Through my heart-pumping pants, I smile. I don't really know why I smile, though.

I turn my attention back to my priorities. I look out the window to notice the moon is high. Even in the middle of the night, the guards are still present.

My body hurts from lying on the wood floor, and my butt is numb.

Charles peers down at me, "What's wrong?"

I lay down on my side to get off my bottom and thighs. I breathe a sigh of relief.

"Are you hurt? Was it from those Mine jerks?"

I pull the sleeve of my shirt to hide the bruises. "Go back to sleep."

Charles stands up eagerly, "I have to go to the bathroom."

"Well, go outside." He scrunches his nose at me in distaste, but I won't give in. It's too risky. "There are no bathrooms close by. So either hold it or find a spot."

"But," Charles turns his head away. "It's the other one," he grumbles.

With a roll of my eyes, I stand. His body will learn to work around school schedule after a week. I take out my knife as we move downstairs. The floor creaks with every step, so at least I'll know if someone springs from the dark.

"Where are we going?"

"Zack's."

I scale the walls, watching every direction, trying to catch any suspicious movement. A team of Boundary members walks by, and I keep us glued to the shadows. They would think we were up to something suspicious and ask questions, and questions come with a poke or a smack.

"What are we doing?"

"Be quiet."

I stop at the last building before calculating our sprint across the open land in front of the school. Zack's is on the opposite side, and his building lights are always on, like a welcoming center.

The barren desert before us seizes my fear. A person heading in that direction has money to spend and, in contrast, money to steal. Despite being neither, faction members of Mine watch from hidden positions prepared to spring upon its victim. I can see their tiny little shadows shifting in the moonlight.

It isn't worth it. Charles can use the bathroom in between

the buildings or something.

I hear whimpers and scuffling as I turn around. It came from the dark side of the alley. Charles heard it too. He stiffens, twisting his head, shifting to peek around the corner.

I know what it is, and I don't want any part of it. I push him back to the door but he doesn't move. "What is it?"

We hear a distinct female's plea, "Leave me alone."

Charles yanks out of my hand and darts to the alley, "Hey!"

I hesitate out of fear. I'm not supposed to go look for trouble; I'm supposed to run away from it. But Charles is swallowed up by the darkness, and I can't see him. This kid is already causing me problems.

"Get out of here, kid," some boy replies.

"Leave her alone," Charles barks back.

I rush into the darkness, snatching hold of his hand and pulling him back to the light, but he struggles against me, digging his feet into the sand and sliding.

He doesn't understand. Bad things happen.

You don't stop it. You don't fight it.

You look away.

Charles wiggles out of my hold and stubbornly turns back to the dark, "Stop being jerks!"

I almost turn to leave.

Don't do anything stupid, remember?

In spite of Tobias, I follow Charles with purpose now, whipping out my knife. I can see the silhouette of two boys standing before a girl. They have her backed up against the wall. She wears a reflective bracelet, a new kid in the neighborhood.

"He said to get away from her," I tell them.

The boys laugh at me, but the girl slips out and runs. They

are uninterested in chasing after her as they turn toward me, "You scared away our friend."

I can make out the guns in a side holster. They are influential members of a clan, and I'm guessing it's Coal considering we are right next to their building. This can't get any worse.

"I wonder what you will do to make it up to us."

"Not a damn thing. Get out of here."

A smile. I can see the white of their teeth in the shadows.

"Don't be like that. Why don't you send the little kid away? We just want to talk to you. What's your name?"

They step closer. I take a step back, but Charles is behind me. He shuffles, and I reach back to grab his arm.

They are closer now. So much closer. The light behind me exposes them while keeping me in the dark. Their faces form into recognizable shapes. One I know from class. I always catch him looking at me. I should know his name, but I can't think of it now.

The left one, the bigger one, reaches out with a careful hand, and I swing at it, lashing at his fingers. He pulls out his gun, "Why do you got to be stupid, girl?"

"You can't shoot me. The rules—"

"Rules? Ash, do you know of any rules?"

Ash, the smaller, familiar one, shakes his head. Now I know who he is. Known famously as Carbon's younger brother and leader of the Coal Empire, he is the worst possible person I could have met tonight.

What should I do? Do I die tonight for nothing? All these months I spent trying to survive, taken by these pieces of shit?

No way.

The bodyguard holds up his gun, surrendering, "Let's talk, girl. Send your little boy away, and let's have a nice chat."

I push Charles out from behind me, slipping the knife to him. He'll need it if I don't come back. "Go to our place." He catches my eyes in the darkness and shakes his head. "Go," I shove him. He trips over himself, leaning against the wall so he won't fall. "Now!" I bark.

Finally, Charles turns and starts running. I release a breath as I face the two of them. They've separated, Ash on my left and his bodyguard on my right. Ash approaches with a smile on his face, "What's your name?" he questions sweetly.

"Fuck you."

He takes one more step, and I slam my fist into his stomach. *So much for Rule Thirteen.*

Ash bends over in pain, and I fold my hands and bring them down on his back. He falls to the floor with a groan, a sound I don't mind. Just as I'm about to kick him, the other kid snatches my hair, yanking me to the floor. The wind knocks from my lungs, and I choke for air.

He puts a foot on my chest, keeping me down, "Who the hell do you think you are, girl? What clan are you from?"

"I'm not part of a stupid clan. But Tobias is going to be pissed if you hurt me."

Now he looks at my arm, finding the black ribbon wrapped around it. He swings his head over shoulder at Ash, "What do you want to do?"

Acne face gets up off his knees. He's still in pain, which is humorous. "Tobias owes me."

"But he'll see this as an insult," the bodyguard assures him.

"Then we'll destroy his clan."

"The Teachers won't let us, and the clan already doesn't think you're a good ruler. I say we let her go. It's not worth it."

"Fuck that. This is *her.* If I have her, the rebellion will be as good as dead, and the clans will thank me."

What rebellion?

The bodyguard examines me, studying my face, contemplating his decision. But I'm not about to leave my fate in his hands. I move to knee the back of his leg when I hear pounding little footsteps on the ground. A sudden whisk of air rushes by me, and bodies smash into the ground. My eyes widened when I see Charles.

He rolls around with the older one, pounding his tiny fists anywhere he can. Ash goes to help, and my fear flings me after him. I grab Ash and kick him between the legs, and he drops with a painful howl. I snatch Charles' shirt, pulling him off the other kid, and together we run fast and hard.

Bullets follow us, echoing in the silent night. I can hear the stray projectiles ricochet off the building and shatter glass in the distance.

I jump through a broken window frame with Charles right behind me. We topple in and roll, but I pick him up and climb numerous stairs till we are all the way at the top and slam the last door in the back.

Without missing a moment, I grab Charles' shirt, panting in his face, "Don't you ever do that. When I tell you to go, you fucking go!" I shove him away, pacing. "Do you know what could have happened? You're so fucking stupid!"

"They were going to hurt you."

"I've already been hurt! I don't need your damned protection. Do you want to die? Do you fucking want to die?"

"No!"

"Then you do what I tell you to do. Do you understand?"

I am breathing so rapidly and heavily I don't feel the tears until they trickle into my mouth. "Fuck!" I scream, wiping my face.

Charles plops on the floor, holding his head in his hands. He cries mutely, his shoulders shaking.

I catch one sight of him, and the guilt creeps in like shadows. But I defend myself, knowing I am not the one in the wrong. I could have gotten away from them. Charles has to know, perhaps not the worst things, but some of the things that could happen. "Clans have the power here. You do exactly what they want and when they want. You don't question. You don't fight it. Unless you want to die. I mean, shit," my fingers twist in my hair with frustration. I throw myself to the floor. Guilt is building, but I need him to understand. "We can survive this place. But we can't be stupid like that."

"They were going to hurt you," he whimpers.

I shuffle beside him and wrap an arm around his shoulders. He leans into me, his body quivering with suppressed sobs. "It's going to happen. People will hurt me. People will hurt you. But the only way to live through it is to take it. Stay alive. That is our main mission. Stay alive."

He sniffles and cries for a few minutes more. My head rests back against the wall. I can still feel the foot on my chest and the fear in my gut. I can't make mistakes. The next time Charles does something stupid, I'll have to run away. I'm not going to risk my survival for him.

Charles snuggles deeper, his body stretching out, and his head rests on my lap.

This kid's gonna kill me.

As my fingers trace his prickly scalp, I close my eyes, no where near ready for sleep. Their voices echo in my head. They spoke about a rebellion. They acted like I had something to do with it. Is that why people look at me? Are they expecting something from me?

"I want to go home. Please." Charles begs, "Please take me home."

"Shh." I whisper in his ear. He's so convinced there's a world out there. It's not a dream or make believe to him despite how I can't fathom a world like his.

But what if it exists?

"Out there," I whisper, "Is it safe?"

He sniffs, and rubs his nose with the back of his hand. "Well, there are bad things that could happen. Getting hit by a car. Someone stealing you. Someone killing you. But there's the police."

"Like Boundary?"

"They're adults. Adults take care of the kids."

"Are they horrible? Like the teachers?"

"Not all of them. My parents are awesome," he looks up at me, "You don't remember your parents?"

I shake my head. "Are you sure I had some?"

"Everybody has parents. Someone that cares for you."

Someone cares for me.

I wipe a tear from my cheek. I stare out the window, finding the walls in the distance. It cuts off any visual to the outside world. It's unfair. I'm so close to the top and still can't see it. But out there, Charles has a family. And maybe I do too.

"I'll get you home."

Charles sits up, wide-eyed and hopeful, "You will? How?"

"We'll escape."

Rule 1: *Do Not Attempt Escape*

"Is that possible?"

"I've never tried. Won't know till we try."

He jumps to his feet, "Let's do it!"

I laugh at his excitement. It's way better than his crying. I'm gonna do what I can to always keep a smile on his face. I'm going to get Charles home.

And maybe me too.

11

Memory

I wake up with the sun. I noticed the sky lighting out of the window we had jumped through. It was around the same time I left the Rain's bathhouse yesterday. I get up without bothering Charles. My limbs are stiff and sore, and it takes a minute for the pain to ease.

The pain makes me bitter and hateful toward Cloud and his friends. If I told on him, what would Drop do? Would it be enough to keep him from attacking me again? Or should I let it go and not think of it?

I make it outside and look toward the alley I had gotten into. I am surprised when the guards that had been there all night are not there now.

I wait patiently, keeping my eye on any changes. It takes a few minutes but finally, new guards exit the Coal compound.

A few minutes every morning, they change posts leaving it unprotected.

Awesome.

There is no way the soldiers would stay for more than eight

to 12-hour shifts. Therefore, between that time, they had to switch again.

Oh, it is too perfect. We can get out before school and after school. It would be our own little world in there.

I can't wait to tell Charles.

I swing around in time to see the face before me. Ruler slams his fist against my head, and I never feel the ground hit me when I fall.

Tobias' hunting party found me.

* * *

Tears spring to my eyes as I wake. I curl into a ball, holding my face. My fingers touch my eye in a desperate attempt to find out if it's still there, but I only cause more pain.

The floor I am on isn't dirt, which grabs my attention. It is Tobias' main room at the Respect Building. I know the carpet better than the back of my hand. It is an ugly, dirty beige with multiple dark spots that were either blood or soda. I glance around and find Ruler sitting in a beat-up green recliner, grinning at me. "You're in trouble," he sings.

Ruler has piercings along his brow, lips, nose, and big dragon-like claws in his ears. He plays with his tongue ring and watches me with hooded green eyes.

Like any Respect member, he is excited by the promise of future violence. His long black hair is tied in a knot at the back of his head. He wears jeans with holes and an oversized gray shirt with a dragon on the front.

Ruler wants to appear like he's in power, but he has bruises, like I do. Seems like I wasn't the only one Rain got ahold of.

I lift my lower body up, my hand continuously cupping my

face despite not helping the pain. "At least I don't look like shit," I bite.

"Who says?"

The door opens, and all of Respect walks in. They look at me briefly, contemplating if they should stay until Tobias walks in. With only a flick of his head, they scatter to their rooms like frightened birds.

Except one.

Kevin kneels down in front of me.

Kevin is mute, and aside from keeping to himself, he hasn't taken part in punishing me. In fact, he usually is the one to care enough to make them stop.

He leans over me, inspecting my face. His brown eyes are full of worry and his gentle face squishes in pity. He reaches out but thinks better of it, looking at Ruler and signing aggressively.

Ruler flicks him off.

I watch Tobias pace. The tiger in the room wants attention.

Kevin grabs an ice pack from the fridge and gently touches my head. I hiss, and his lips smush together in an apology.

"Leave her. She's had worse." That is Tara, of course.

"Get out," Tobias orders his three remaining sidekicks. Ruler is disappointed he doesn't get to partake in my torment this time while Tara wiggles her fingers at me with a giddy smile. Kevin reluctantly leaves after making me hold the ice pack.

Tobias stops before me, towering above me as I kneel on the floor. "What happened?"

"With what?"

"Don't you play dumb," he unhooks his whip from its place on his side. The tail unrolls and drops to the floor. The sight of it sets panic in my heart, "I'm tracked down by Coal members. Saying you attacked the leader of Coal and his guard."

I hang my head.

Fucking liars.

I look up, unwilling to defend myself, when it's apparent he's already decided to punish me.

"Let me fill you in on politics here, baby, because I don't think you're getting it. You are at the bottom of the cesspool. An ant insignificant to the structure here. You don't matter. The only reason you've been saved from Auction time and time again is because I keep you here. So when you do fucked up shit, it looks bad on me. I risk my reputation for you."

"Don't."

He cackles, but it's heavy, full of rage. He kneels down in front of me. "You want to go to Auction? Do you know what it means?"

With a bowed head, I admit I don't.

"You are put on a stage in front of people. And they bid on you."

I snap my eyes up.

"They decide your price based on your performance here. Based on your spirit. On your obedience," he touches the side of my face, "On your virginity."

I sneer as I twist away, but Tobias grabs my chin, forcing me to meet his eyes. "If you get sold, they own you. If you don't, you get killed, and your body parts are split up and sold. Either way, someone is making money off you."

I shove him off me. He told me once Auction leads kids off a cliff to be burned alive, and now he comes up with another story. "I don't believe you," I attempt to get to my feet, but Tobias digs his nails into my arm.

"I don't care. But you will obey me. Do not go to Coal's Territory again. I lied to them. I told them you were with me last night, and it couldn't possibly have been you. I've bought myself some time till I can fix this shit, but if-*when* Ash realizes I've lied to him, he'll tell the principal, and if that man gets involved, we're done." Tobias stands up with his whip sliding across the floor like a rattlesnake, waiting to strike. He walks to the front window, looking out as if there's a battalion out there now.

"Why did you lie?" I stand with my hands fisted at my side. "If I'm nothing, why did you lie? Why risk anything?" He ignores me, but I'm tired of my questions not being answered. "Is it because of Memory?"

He turns his head upon the name.

"The rebellion?"

"The rebellion is dead," Tobias peers at the camera in the corner. "And so is she."

Why does he look there and not at me?

"You don't believe that."

He scoffs, turning to me, "Don't tell me what I believe. Memory was a liar, and she betrayed everyone. So don't talk about shit you know nothing about," he snaps the whip at the lamp, knocking it over.

The crash kickstarts my heart, and I back up.

"You owe me, Scream. Coal could kill me for this," he snaps the whip again, slicing it into a pillow. The cotton falls out like snow. He fastens to me so quickly I stumble as I back up, but he catches my arm, "When you're healed, I want you to come to me. I'm tired of fighting you." With the whip still in his hand, he presses his palm against the side of my face, holding me still as he kisses me. I squeeze my mouth shut against his harsh grip. Tobias rests his forehead against mine, his touch now gentle, like the soft caress of a spider. "I care about you.

I'll keep you safe, but I need you to listen to me." When he pulls back, he finally acknowledges the welt over my eye. He sneers and calls out, "Ruler!"

I'm released back into the campus. I was a caged rabbit, and now I'm running without thinking about where to go. I'm so pathetic because of my fear. I hate how much Tobias affects me.

I force myself to stop, resting my hands on my knees as I breathe.

Charles.

With my mind clear, I observe the sand-covered lands. It's early morning, and some clan members are beginning to set up their little wooden stands. I walk back the way I ran, feeling the confused gazes of the kids I passed.

Charles, where are you?

How can he survive without me? Would somebody try to hurt him? He is too precious for this place. People would see that and try to destroy him, as they were destroying me. I must find him.

"Scream!"

My body whirls around, and I spot him running towards me from the playground. He is smiling, coming to a stop, but I pull him into a hug, "Are you okay? Are you hurt?"

"I'm fine, but what about you? What happened to your face? Who did that?" He struggles to pull away, but I don't want him to look at it.

"It's fine. Are you hungry?"

He nods into my chest. "Are you sure you're okay?"

"I'm fine. Don't you worry about me." I grab his face between my palms, "If I disappear, you stay hidden until Harvest. Fight your way into a clan. Do not try to find me."

"Don't go anywhere, and I won't look for you."

I kiss his peace fuzz head, and hand in hand, we walk to the market alley where the cafe is. I don't want to talk about it anymore, but Charles still has questions.

"That wasn't because of me, was it?"

"No. Stop worrying about it."

"Why would someone hurt you? You're so nice."

"I'm not so nice."

"You have to be nice. You saved me. And you saved that girl."

If only he knew I almost ran away.

When we get to the cafe, Zack is quick to put ice on my eye. I hiss and curse at him, which he only laughs at. I swat his hands, but Charles grabs my fingers to stop me.

I sit there trying to ignore the guards behind Zack, standing like vigils. A six-foot Asian teenager on the verge of manhood and another boy barely pubescent, quiet, motionless, staring ahead dressed in all white.

"What's wrong with them?" Charles asks to my horror. I 'tsk' at him, but Zack heard it.

He smiles, "Nothing. They're my Specials."

"Specials?"

"They all have special talents. Jam-Jam knows Jin-jitzu. Glass can strike a target a hundred yards out. You know, things like that."

"Why would you need that?"

Zack smiles wide with a hint of false softness, "There's a war going on, sweet boy. There's always a war."

Someone calls for Zack, and he hops to his feet, leaving us. The Specials follow behind him like shadows. People get silent, observing as they pass by. It's haunting because here we all are in this insane world, and yet there is a wave of pity hanging over us like a dark cloud. We pity them as if their world is any worse than ours.

Charles nudges me with quiet questions, but I don't have answers for him.

Throughout the day, I watch, trying to find signs of a building rebellion. Ash commented the rebellion would die if he could get rid of me.

But why? What do I have to do with it? How am I connected to Memory?

And Zack's cryptic message, 'There's always a war.'

When school gets out, I meet Charles at the gates. Tobias doesn't acknowledge me; still upset about this morning.

We go to the cafe to eat. Charles has so much to say about his day. It shifts from subject to subject faster than I can keep up, but when he talks about his home and school beyond the walls, all my attention is on him, spellbound. I want to hear every detail. I try to imagine it, a place that isn't here. I use pictures from my history books, images of grass and trees, mountains, and rivers. With his words as a guide, I know life exists outside the walls. It's real. There is more hope in me than ever before. I can get out of here. If there are ways in, there are ways out. The teachers want us to believe escape isn't possible, that there is no life outside, but Memory made it out. I believe it, like the little boy Tobias destroyed.

I believe it.

And whether she's alive right now doesn't matter. She made it out, and so can I.

12

The Wastelands

I lead us out of the cafe as the sun begins to sink. "It's time to learn how to make money."

"Money?" Charles scrunches his nose.

"Tickets. To buy anything, you need tickets. And what I do is go to the Wastelands." I point my finger across the barren land in front of the school. It isn't a difficult time to cross, so now will be a perfect chance to get over there.

As we approach, Charles' enthusiasm begins to falter. I am already dragging him, so I get aggravated when his feet stop moving. I turn, finding his green eyes filled with fear.

"Charles."

He shakes his head, backing up. Anyone could be watching out in the open like this, waiting to jump on us. He's making me nervous.

"I don't, I don't want to go there."

"Charles, you have too."

"No," his sight shifts to catch my eye, "Please, Scream. I don't want to go there."

"It's not so bad," I assure. Charles continues to shake his head, trying to back up. I take both his hands in mine and kneel down. "I wouldn't take you here if there was anything else to do. But this is the only way to earn tickets. Do you understand?"

"There has to be another way," he turns to go, but I snatch his hand.

"Do you want to kill?" Panic shakes his head. "Do you want to shoot someone in the head?" He tries to get my fingers off him. "Do you want to beat the shit out of some little kid as he begs you to stop?" Tears are spilling down his cheeks in frustration. "Then this is the only option."

Compassion isn't an easy thing. Months in this place have beaten down my compassion, layers upon layers of fear and hate built on it, keeping it buried. Two days of knowing this kid, I am on my knees, looking into his watery green eyes. "I'll be here with you."

With his little fingers in mine, we walk to the Wasteland.

The smell is harsh, and Charles holds his nose with the silliest expression of disgust scrunching his lips. His bare feet squish in the vile mud, "Ah, yuck!" yet he continues through, finding footholes to climb the pile of trash. "My sister would be squealing like a pig."

"What's her name?"

"Zuri."

It's a better name than Scream. Would he mind if I stole it?

His fingers slip out of my hand as he darts up the hill, standing at the top. "This is the grossest thing I've done. And I've done some gross things."

It is amazing how someone could find wonder in even the illest of places.

He is amazing, my little brother.

I laugh as I chase after him. We tumble and throw trash, dodging and catching. "You missed." I tease. He pounces on me, hitting me in my stomach playfully. "You're as weak as a newborn. Come here," I pull him over to a more stable area and grab his hand. "Fold your fingers like this," I make a fist, and he mimics. "You punch like this," I demonstrate. "So there is weight behind it. Your body weight is more powerful than just your arm strength." I wiggle his arm, "You got puny little arms. I want you to do thirty pushups every day."

"You can do that much?"

"I do fifty."

"NO way, you're lying." I punch him in the arm. He grimaces and rubs the spot.

"I don't lie."

We get back to searching. It takes a few hours, and with multiple playful interruptions, we have enough to feed us through the weekend.

As we head to the checkout, I whisper to him, "When we get out. Run and run hard."

"Why?"

"Why do you think, dummy. People are going to try to take our money. Do you want to eat tonight or not?"

"Yes, I'm starving!"

"You remember what I told you about our hideout?"

"Wait till the guards go inside. Scale one side of the building, and make sure I'm not being watched. Then turn in, run down the alley, make another right, and I'm home."

Home. That's exactly what it will be for us.

"Good, but now let's meet at the cafe." I push him out first. I want to keep after him, to protect him, but he must do this alone. He will learn what it means to fail. It is cold and ruthless, but that is precisely how he needs to become.

He gets his money and tucks it in a safe place, takes one look back at me for encouragement, then shoots off in a sprint. I peek out to see bald children chasing after him. I give up my possessions, only receiving five tickets.

I start to take off in the opposite direction but damn it to hell, if I don't run straight in the direction he took off in. I hear the footsteps following me, but the only fear I have now is if Charles hadn't been able to get away.

What would I do about it? I don't kill, I don't fight. I run.

I am stupid. I shouldn't have let Charles go off on his own. He doesn't know the streets like I do. I have had months of practice, and he's only been here a few short days. I push more into my feet. I shouldn't have let him go.

A scream, and I swing right. Charles is on the ground, getting beaten up by three little kids. Senseless, I run full flight into them, slamming into one, and his body flings backward into the sand. I swing out a right hook, knocking a child in the face, and they're down and out.

I kneel down to Charles, whimpering on the ground. I touch his arm, and he glimpses at me with tears. I reach for him, wrapping his arm around my shoulder, but as I get up, I realize there are new arrivals. A group of Mine Members circling us like a pack of hyenas.

"Remember me?" The tallest boy replies. He's got a bruise on his cheek, which I'm pretty sure I gave him. The boy next to him has white gauze over his broken nose, and I'm pretty sure I did that too.

I drop Charles back on the ground and face them. I beat them once; I can do it again. There are more of them than last time, but I have better confidence than before. I have someone to protect, and I can't lose.

I take a step forward, but a gun goes off nearby. We scatter like bats in the light. I grab Charles, pulling him off the dirt floor. He gets to his feet, and we sprint to the closest Rat building.

I am huffing for air. The adrenaline is pumping through my veins. Charles lands on the wood ground, crying now.

Rage fills me.

He can't be weak forever. He needs to fight!

"I want to go home," Charles cries into his hands. "I want to go home. Please, please take me home."

"Enough."

"I'm sorry for everything. Just take me home. Please, please just take me home."

How often have I wished someone was there for me to cry too? How often did I cry, wanting to leave this place even if this world was all there was?

I drop to my knees. My rage being reduced with each of Charles' wails.

He is only a kid, girl. Just a child. I am older, wiser, and not innocent or naive.

Charles is what I lost. I grab him and hug him, squeezing to the point of pain. "It's okay," I whisper. "I'm here."

I want to protect him. I will protect him like I need to be protected. And to do that, I might have to hurt people. But that's okay. I'll be bad so he can be good. If we ever get out of here, he'll be pure, innocent, and welcomed back into his family. I'll make sure of it.

13

Harvest

At seven precisely, the guards leave their post. I grab Charles' small hand, and we run down the alleyway. He plops down in the sand, lying with his arms and legs spread wide. I keep my eyes on the entrance wondering if anyone saw us.

"Come on, we made it," Charles calls over. I swing back and put a finger to my lips. Call me paranoid, but I sit against the wall watching, waiting for someone to come find us or steal our secluded spot for themselves. I have a nagging feeling someone is watching me again.

"So, how long have you been here?" he asks me. I'm sure by now he's already bored. This kid is hard to handle. He never wants to sit and enjoy the quiet.

"Three months."

And four days.

"That's crazy. So there's really no way out."

My eye goes to him. It's hard for me to understand what

goes on in his head because he is so young and new to this world. He smiles a ton, makes jokes, and constantly searches for something to entertain him. I don't realize he is struggling as I am.

"The front doors have a whole set of doors behind it. They open twice a month. One is for Shipment, and it comes on the last Saturday of the month. Then in two weeks, it will open again."

"Why?"

"They take children to…"

The Reaping. Auction. I never understood it before. There was a time I thought I wanted to go. I even told Tobias to let me. He laughed at me. "Stupid girl," he said. "They drive you into a pit of fire. Would you like to know how it feels to be burned alive? I can show you."

"They take kids." I cut myself off and changed the subject. "I've circled the whole place following the wall." I touch it now, staring up as it stretches like a black hole. It seems endless, being so close to it. "There is no other door. But I've never been in the clan houses. There might be a way out through there."

Charles eyes the wall, "What if we dig?" He drops to his knees, burying his hands into the sand.

I laugh at first, but it doesn't stop his attempt. I've never thought about digging. I kneel beside him, monitoring, perhaps even hoping a miracle will occur.

"I'm gonna need a shovel," he proclaims. "I used to dig holes at the beach."

"Beach?" I've only seen a beach in my history book. Instead of a wall, it's a vast landscape of water. It sounds like heaven. "We'll buy you one in the market tomorrow morning."

Charles sits back, knocking the sand from his hands. "Why don't you remember anything?"

I rest against the wall, "I don't know."

"Maybe you were in an accident."

"What kind of accident?"

"A car accident? Or you fell out of a tree house or something and banged your head."

"You think…" I pause, dusting my pants to keep the emotion out of my voice, "You really think I have a home?"

"Well, yeah." He gets up on his knees again to start digging, but sneaks a peek at me and sneers, "Your eye looks so messed up."

I throw sand at him.

* * *

Every day adds a little more happiness. I didn't know I knew how to smile or laugh. Charles is a one-man show, a spotlight following him, and I'm his one-kid audience, applauding everything he does. For a nine-year-old, he knows so much. He befriends so many kids that I get jealous when he waves to someone or stops to talk. It's frustrating how quickly he's involved in other people's lives. I want to believe it's a danger to me, to us, but he ignores me when I warn him of the awful things that could happen if he gets too close to someone. He attempts to get me into conversations with strangers, but I remain silent and cold. I don't need anyone else but Charles.

I turn from a group of his friends, deciding I'd rather be alone, but it isn't long before he calls after me. I slow my pace for his little legs.

"You know," he begins, "People talk about you."

"I don't care."

"There are rumors."

About the rebellion?

I think about asking, but I'm afraid he's heard some not nice things about me because of Tobias. I don't want Charles to know what I've been through. "I don't care."

"Why do you want to be alone?"

I don't.

"Because people are monsters."

He sighs and gives up.

I swing at him, "I've been here a lot longer than you, so drop it."

"I've dropped it, jeez."

I punch him and run, and he is quick to chase me. This is what I want. Just him and me. All these other people are thorns. They prick without warning.

We go to Zack's Cafe for breakfast. The bathroom here is small, meant for two people at most. It smells of lavender. There are lotions on the counters and hairbrushes in a round cylinder. I brush my hair with water, getting all the knots out while I stare vehemently at my face. Despite how bad my eye was, all that's left is a dark ring around it and it's slowly fading. I'm healing. I repeat that little mantra in my head because I must be healing. I'm different in a way I didn't know I could be.

I can't remember who I was or how I was before this world, but each day I'm with Charles, little pieces of my shattered existence repair itself. I have a sense of humor. I have courage. I have confidence.

I don't know if it was there all along, but I do know I like it. I want more of it.

I sit beside Charles, eating as he talks about a random cartoon show he likes.

The intercom comes on. A young female voice interrupts all the conversations. "All kids with a wristband must head to the field now. Harvest begins in one hour."

Charles looks down at his wrist, "Hey, where'd mine go?"

Guilt makes me reply briskly, "It's not fun, so you're not missing out."

"Harvest. That's what the posters on the school walls are all about. But what is it exactly?"

The weekend following a shipment, clans chose new recruits to join their ranks. A kid with a wristband is forced to go whether they want to or not. Boundary scouts out any stragglers.

Rats, people that have been kicked out of their clan since last month, or kids that didn't get snatched for Auction are forced to participate. I'm technically a Rat, and I'm supposed to participate in Harvest, but like Tobias loves to remind me, he keeps me safe from Auction. It's one of the reasons why I don't do more to stop him. I need him even if I hate him.

Charles gets excited because it is something to do to pass the time. I try at first to deny him, thinking he'll realize what I have done. But Charles is, if nothing else, persistent.

The stadium is in the top corner of our world. We walk in through the doors with everyone else. Unlike when I come in at night, the place is packed with kids. Inside are big metal bleachers traveling up at least sixty feet. Students congregate, separated by clans. Boundary soldiers line up on the rail, keeping an eye out for any fights.

With nearly a hundred people out on the fields, the stands are full, probably bringing our numbers between five to six hundred.

"There are a lot of kids," Charles comments. With the town being so large, it doesn't feel like there are enough of us but in moments like this, when we are all packed together, it's undeniable there are too many kids here.

Charles races up the bleachers, dodging between bodies like a football player running to the endzone. I chase him, clamping my lips tight to stop from calling out. My anxiety is at an all time high. He only stops when he's at the top. I snatch his hand, quietly scolding him as I pull him to sit.

"So what clan is what?"

We sit above Boundary because it is easy to remain unseen in their vast numbers. They wear red and yellow artifacts, masks, painted faces, waving flags, and foamed fingers. Sitting in a raised box, their leaders are at the base of their section, but I'm not privy to their names.

Coal is across from us, dressed in black and gray. They have similar items like Boundary waving erratically as if this is a fun sport and not a violent life and death tournament.

Coal's four top members sit at the center. Ash is dominant, and though I can't make out his face, I know it. The acne, the sunken cheeks, the pointed chin, and his oily hair. He dresses in black cargo pants too big for him and a dark shirt with the clan's sigil on the front. He moves his gaze toward the crowd, searching for someone.

I shrink, hoping it's not me.

Rain sits beside Coal, contrasting beautifully against Coal's dark colors. Somehow I manage to find Light in all this madness. He's like a willow tree in a swamp. Drop stands beside him. I envy her in the way a peasant does a god. It's nothing close to hate and much more love than is good for you.

Standing the highest among the Rain Clan is Hail.

What if he's part of the rebellion? Does he think I have something to do with it and that's why he saved me?

To the left are the smaller clans. Respect, Spread, and Sky. There are fifty people between the three of them. Zack sits on yellow and purple bean bags and has a drink in his hand while the other holds his enormous round hat on his head.

"What's Sky?" Charles wonders.

They are dressed in black ninja outfits and are the oddest looking bunch out in the hot sun. Sky's clan lives on the rooftops, and they do not mess with us 'ground dwellers'. To be a part of it, one has to be fearless of heights, have superb upper body strength, and have no humanity. Sky members are all Snatchers. They steal kids in the middle of the night that got on a teacher's bad side and are never seen again.

Tobias is the conductor of this whole charade, and when he comes to the center of the field, the crowd yells for him in praise. I snicker when I hear several 'boos' as well. He divides the kids into twenty-five, making it an even number of wristbands and others.

It doesn't take Charles long to figure out why I hate this event when the contest starts. His excitement dwindles until he sits beside me in silence, barely looking at what is happening before us.

At first, no one wants to fight. The kids with wristbands haven't figured this world out yet. They look at each other and everyone around them, wondering what they should do.

The protagonists come from the Rats or a person attempting to switch clans. Their desperation turns the event into a brawl shortly enough. Changing clans isn't easy, and there are certain rules to it I'm not clear on.

As for a Rat, well, it's life or death.

The clans watch, judging who has the best fighting skills, who can be taught, and who will become an asset to their clan. It's not about winning, really. A kid can be beaten almost to death, but they will get chosen and saved if they put up a commendable fight.

The more blood, the more excitement builds. It's like gladiators in Roman times but with kids instead of full-grown adults. It makes it much worse.

I look at Charles, "You ready to go?"

He nods quietly, and we leave the stands before the end can arrive.

Usually, I would stay in my own head, thinking about the handful of children that will die today. But my eyes slip to Charles, flicking over to him every so often to see if his face has changed.

I don't like him so quiet. I nudge him, and he doesn't bother to nudge back. "Talk to me," I say. I want to know what he's thinking, and I want to know if it's the same as inside my own.

"If we escape, we would be leaving everyone behind."

"What's your point?"

Charles looks back to the Harvest field, walking backward, "They're stolen, like us."

"You don't know that. The teachers said their parents didn't want them."

He swings around, "My parents wanted me."

"Didn't you fight your dad? Wasn't he mad at you?"

"That doesn't mean he doesn't want me anymore. People fight, and I get in trouble a lot, but my mom still loves me."

"How do you know?"

"Because I know."

I shrug, not willing to push. He's upset enough. We pass members of Boundary dressed in red. Charles pins his gaze on their guns. He's fascinated and yet scared.

"We have to save them."

"Save them?" I laugh more than I probably should. This whole conversation is so far out of my thoughts I can't even fathom what he means. "What are you talking about?"

"This place is screwed up. No one belongs here. Not you and not them."

I tuck hair behind my ear as I mumble, "Some of them belong here."

"Scream. This place isn't right."

I throw up a hand, "We can't even save ourselves! I don't know what you think you can do, but you are a little kid. This world would destroy you if I wasn't around."

Why did that sound like something Tobias would say?

"Let's find people like us. We can start our own clan."

I laugh in bewilderment.

"There are others out there that want to go home too."

I stop and meet his face. He's being too serious about something that's impossible. "They may want to go home, but they like it here. Do you?" My temper is rising. I could hear the beat of my heart. I didn't want him to change my plans. Saving ourselves is something plausible and attainable. But now he's talking about more people? How?

"We could fix this place. Stop kids from dying. Help the weak ones survive-"

"If you want to do all that, then fine, join a clan." I shun him, turning to get away from him.

He comes after me. "I don't want to join a clan. They are all screwed up. You said so yourself."

"How do you expect us to start a clan? We don't have tickets. We don't have guns. We don't have anything."

"We don't need anything. Just us is good enough."

I shake my head. "It's more complicated than that."

"No, it's not. Look, you helped me, and I'm here because of that. What if we help someone else and they stay? And then we help another person, and they stay?"

"We can't help anyone, Charles." I laugh at him, raising my voice in hysteria. "You don't get it. Tobias won't allow it."

"Who's Tobias?"

"He's..."

He's nobody.

Why did that thought come into my head? What power does he have over me that he would be in this conversation?

I have grown accustomed to what I can and cannot do based on Tobias' tastes. I'm losing myself more than I already have by conforming to him.

I have become exactly what he wants.

The rebellious temper in me rises.

"Let's do it."

His green gaze brightens like the sun. "Really?" I assure him, and he jumps at me in a hug. "Awesome. The first thing we need is a name."

He goes on blubbering. I watch him with interest. He really has a fanciful imagination. He hastily picks out random titles like "The Rangers", "Iron Maidens," or my favorite, "Spider Fighters."

He's an odd one, but he's mine.

14

My Place

Before the sun rises, I nudge Charles awake. He groans at me but sits up with a giant yawn to fill his lungs. I crack a smile. "The guards will be switching out. We have to go."

It is a simple escape, and I release a breath of fear. I know my home is too good to be true so I'm waiting for that moment when someone sees us.

We hold hands as we walk. He swings my arm exaggeratedly. He hums a tune, his happiness soaks into me, and I don't stop my smile when it spreads on my lips.

So swiftly, he blurts out, "I think someone's watching us."

I stop. My momentary lapse of fear now surges like a tidal wave. I've been feeling the same for a while, but I thought it was my personal paranoia. I examine the rooftops.

What if it's Snatchers? What if we're being sold? How can I stop such a thing? How can I fight it? Do we need to leave the hideout? Where else will we be safe? There's no unknown cave, no hidden room. How can I keep him safe?

Charles shakes my shoulders, "Hello!" he's giggling, "I don't think they're evil. I think they're protecting us."

I scoff, inspecting the rooftops. "You were probably dreaming. What do you want for breakfast?" The thought however doesn't stray from my mind. I'll have to keep a look out.

After we eat, we head to school. I notice Tobias standing with Tara and a bunch of other members of Respect by the entrance steps. His eyes catch me, and he smiles. My stomach twitches in sickness. His gaze lowers to the boy on my arm, and I notice it darken with that hidden rage I know so well. I break loose of Charles, "Head to class," He looks up at me, unsure but does as I say.

I meet Tobias on the side of the steps. A ripped poster hangs up behind him advertising for Coal. 'Embrace the Dark,' it reads in black letters dripping with fire. 'Show your brutal fighting skills at Harvest and join the elite.'

"Who was that?" Tobias asks, reaching out his hand for mine. I don't move. "No one."

He snags my fingers, pulling me to him. "I haven't seen you all weekend." Tobias kisses my cheek, touching the bruise Ruler gave me. "Still hurt?" He presses into it, and I twist away with a wince. Tobias laughs, "Guess so." He wraps his arm around my shoulders and directs me toward his group. "Did you go to the Harvest?"

Unfortunately.

"No."

"You missed a ton of fun. I got a new one." He tips his head over to the new recruit against the wall. "Named him Hammer. He bulldozed a whole freaking lot of them. Had to pay top dollar for him, but he's ours."

The kid he speaks of plays with a basketball going in and

out between his enormous legs. He's thick in body, with big hands and round arms. He passes the ball off to Kevin before turning his dark brown eyes onto me.

My interest dies off. I don't care about his new pet.

Tara catches my attention and winks at me. She sits on a wooden crate with her legs crossed, her platform shoe waving as she wags her leg.

"Look who it is," Ruler stands up from the wall, tossing his cigarette. He steps out in front of us, and Kevin grabs his arm. Ruler snaps out of it but doesn't move any closer.

Drop approaches like a goddess on a pedestal. She walks as if the sun shines only for her. Her hair is perfectly brushed and curled as it sways with each step. Beside her and holding her hand is Hail. He's a foot taller than her and entirely out of her league in appearance. He's a peasant beside such beauty.

Members of Rain form like a cumulus behind her, a mass of white shirts spreading across the horizon. Light is in the group, and for a second, our eyes meet, but his attention goes to Tobias, and his features alter into disgust. Within the crowd as well is Cloud. He hangs back, smirking as he sees us. He doesn't say anything, afraid Hail or Drop might hear him, but he touches his face, the three scratches on his cheek, and winks at me.

Ruler bucks, but Tara has his arm. "Fucking asshole," he curses, turning his back as the crowd trickles inside. Ruler pins his brown eyes on Tobias, "What are you going to do about them? It's been a week since they attacked us, and you've done nothing. If you don't have the balls, tell me, and I'll get my own revenge."

Tobias lights up a cigarette. He takes his time, making sure the paper catches. He sucks it in, and ashes appear on the tip.

He blows it out slowly, till the air clears. He steps up close to Ruler, and I sink back. I wish the sand would suck me up.

"I got a plan," Tobias murmurs. "Give me your hand."

Ruler nervously glances at us as if any of us would help. "Why?"

Tobias doesn't answer, taking another drag and blowing it in his face.

My heart pounds, and I use the wall for comfort. Ruler rubs his mouth and looks over his shoulder, searching for the time, but school isn't starting for another two minutes. With a bout of courage or anger, Ruler puts his hand out, and it shakes, but he folds it into a fist to hide it.

Tobias eyes his cigarette, how the tip of it burns and smoke rises from it. My breath increases with every passing second, trying to prepare myself for what he's gonna do, but I'm not immune or desensitized as I should be. I hate violence.

I hate everything about this place.

Tobias flicks the cigarette over Ruler's shoulder. There is a wave of relief that passes through us, even Tara releases tension from her body. Tobias leans in with a hand on Ruler's neck, "Don't. Try. Me." He enunciates with a squeeze. Tobias pulls away and slaps Ruler's arm with a fake friendliness, "Let's go to class."

I put a hand over my mouth, the adrenaline making me nauseous. Ruler runs a hand through his greasy hair as he backs up, "Yeah." He embarrassingly turns without looking at us and hurries away.

Tobias rotates toward us with a smug smile, "Dick."

Tara giggles, "He was about to pee his pants." She rubs Tobias' arm, kissing him on the cheek. She's like a puppy trying to get attention. "You're so hot when you're mad."

Tobias adores the praise, and he eyes me, hoping for the same. He brushes Tara's hand off his chest and steps up to me. "Did you see him shake?"

Tara lingers behind him, and I watch over his shoulder as she sneers at me. I'd do anything to pass off his attention, and she'd do anything to get it. As much as she claims we are the same, this is a glaring sign that we are anything but.

Tara goes into the school, leaving me alone with Tobias. As much as I hate her, I wish she would have stayed. Not that I would expect her to save me or stop Tobias, but it wasn't as lonely.

"Are you proud of yourself?" I bite.

I'm emotionally drained, and it's only the beginning of the day.

Tobias puts his hands on my hips. "Oh, baby, I had to put him in his place." He touches the side of my face, and I turn my head, swallowing the bile in my throat. His fingers slip into my hair, and my eyes widen, "Your turn," and he grabs it in a fist. I give a sharp cry as he twists my head up to look at him, "What's with you and that kid?"

"Nothing," I quickly assure him, putting my hands on his chest. "Please. School is going to start."

"School starts when I say it does."

I move to knee him in the groin, but Tobias backs up at the last second, laughing.

"You think I don't know your tricks by now?" he mocks, holding me tight. "I'll let you go after you tell me where you are hiding? I sent Ruler out for you, and he couldn't find you. You're staying away from Coal like I told you?"

The lie is quick off my tongue, "Zack let me stay with him."

"Don't," his playful mood dissolves instantly, and I don't know if it's concern or displeasure that replaces it. "Don't go near Zack."

"Anyone is safer than you." I yank away, a few pieces of hair pulled from my scalp. I run up the stairs, careless if I bump into anyone.

I grip the edge of my desk, a pathetic attempt to strengthen myself against the rage inside me. I'm so tired of dealing with his erratic mood swings.

Tobias enters the class, nodding to a few friends as he saunters closer. I want to be invisible, but it's too late.

He always finds me.

Tobias leans over me, his tattooed hands on the desk, touching my fingers. "Let's not fight, huh?" He pulls at my hand tenderly.

I fold only because I fear what will happen if I don't. He pulls me to my feet and wraps me into a tight hug with his mouth at my ear. "You can keep your little doll. He's too young to do anything for you anyway."

"It's not like that," I hiss.

He tightens his hold to an almost painful embrace. My nails dig in his bicep fearfully. "You're mine, beautiful. Make sure you behave. It's Reaping Week."

15

Reaping Week

Rule 11: Reaping Will be the Second Friday of Every Month

Reaping week: five days of teachers deciding who goes up for Auction. Some of them have a point system. Others go off on how they are feeling that week. All they have to do is write down a name and the Snatchers come for you at night.

Miss Nancy waddles in. Her fat feet can't even fit in shoes anymore. She wears slippers, and they slide across the floor with a 'shhing' sound. She wheezes, reaching for the desk. Her flower ankle-length dress sways with each step like a pendulum. She's the fattest person I've ever seen. I guess teachers don't have to scrape for food.

She plops in the chair with exhaustion and scrutinizes us, daring anyone to say something about it. From her bag, she slaps a black notebook on the table. We sit quietly, uneasily, never fully ready for what she has to say.

"Who can tell me about Ted Bundy?"

A hand goes up, "He killed a bunch of people."

"Very vague, Peat," Miss Nancy curls a lip. "Need I remind

you what week it is? The best time of the month." Her disgust turns into a delighted smile as she sits back. "I'll give you one more chance. Do you want to do better than that?"

I sneak a glance at the boy. He sits at his desk in a black polo, balancing on the back of the chair, and it snaps down on the floor as he stutters in response. He looks to his friends, other Coal members, but they keep their heads down, suddenly not so supportive.

"I'm…" Peat swallows, "I'm a Coal Leader. I don't participate in the Reaping."

"I'm a teacher," Miss Nancy mischievously grins. "If I want you in the Reaping, you'll be in the Reaping. So do you want to try again?"

The teacher's pet is finally getting a bit of his own medicine. I love it.

"He…he um…kidnapped, raped, and murdered a few dozen women around the country."

"How did he get away with it?"

"He was…Nice?"

Miss Nancy nods and writes something down. We watch the shift in her hand as if we can tell from here what she's writing. "No one is above the Reaping," she pops her head up, and I turn away. "Let's keep that in mind this week, shall we?"

I forgot to tell Charles about this week. If he were in a clan, they would have warned him. I need to do better. He's my responsibility.

Class is more stressful than usual. I'm afraid to move, afraid to answer. We aren't allowed bathroom breaks during the six hours of school, but Miss Nancy takes three, giving us a little reprieve from her surveillance. Even then, we aren't entirely unwatched. The red dot continues to blink on the camera in the corner.

In the beginning, I never took notice of the cameras. I didn't understand it. But now, when I glare at it, I'm glaring at whoever is watching. They're as bad as the teachers, if not worse, because there are things they see that the teachers don't, and they still stay silent behind their screens.

Five more minutes, and school will be over.

"You."

It's quiet, and I raise my head, searching for the person Miss Nancy called upon. Then I notice her eyes are on me.

"Stand up."

Dread builds like a thunderstorm, moving in with a speed that can't be outrun. I obey, standing, my fingertips idling on the wood of my desk for a molecule of support.

"Who was Jeffery Dahmar?"

Blood drains from my face, "I don't know."

"Who was Marylin Manson?"

"I don't know," My knees shake and now my hand lays on the wood, attempting to keep me from falling.

"Who was Yang Xinhai?"

"I don't know."

"Who is Mickey Mouse?"

A wave of cackles creep up behind me and I flush with embarrassment. "He's a mouse."

Miss Nancy sweetly smiles, "Well, look at that. You know something." She drops her head and writes something in the notebook. Once more, I'm staring at her writing as if I could tell the shape of my name from here.

When the bell rings, I drop in my chair. The wave of adrenaline leaves me sick and I swallow the building saliva in my mouth. A headache isn't too far behind and I rest my forehead on the desk, enjoying the coolness. I would love to cut off my skin and become someone else for a while.

I hate her as much as I hate Tobias.

Miss Nancy is manipulating, teaching us about all the evil that exists. She and Tobias are a team in their influence to keep me from seeking an escape. If Charles wasn't constantly talking about the fun he has out there, I would never want to leave this world. Even with the monsters that live here.

As horrible as this place is, I know it like the back of my hand. I know how to spot evil here, and I can handle what comes at me. I know how to protect Charles and myself. But if we get out, how will I be able to keep him safe? I won't know what's dangerous. Or who.

A hand drops on my shoulder. Terror blares in my brain. I kick out of my desk, falling over on top of it. It smacks the ground making my ears ring, and my head bangs against the teacher's desk as I fall forward. I roll onto my back, holding my head, and search for my attacker.

When I look up, Light hides his eyes and shakes his head.

My embarrassment spreads over my face.

"Jeezes, girl. I'm the last person you should be afraid of," he grumbles with that annoying tone he uses with me. His hand reaches out in offer. His blue eyes are not as friendly as he tries to appear.

When I place my hand in his, it is swallowed by his massive fingers. They are thick and powerful and so well cleaned, and I am afraid just by touching me, he'll dirty himself.

With little effort on both our parts, he lifts me as easily as one of these plastic chairs. Being so near to him, his height towers over me. He is a head and a half taller than me and just as thick. I am a starving anorexic, and he is a well-fed bodybuilder. If we were any more opposite, I would be some stray cat meowing for food.

I take a step back, but I bump into the desk.

He sounds irritated and backs up, "Look, you need to stay away from Tobias." It isn't a warning. He orders it like he has any right to do so.

The absurdity of the demand makes me laugh, and I cover my mouth, surprised by the outburst. It's only what I've been trying to do since the first day I got here. "Great idea," I quip before turning to go.

Light reaches for my arm, but I smack his fingers, taking a step back.

He holds up his hand, "Sorry."

"Don't touch me."

"Can you listen to me, please?"

"Why? Who the hell are you?"

"I want to be your friend."

I'm once more blown out of the water. I couldn't be any more confused if someone picked me up and dropped me on the moon.

Light grabs the desk, sets it right and rests his hands on it. But he shifts again, crossing his arms over his chest. And even then, he doesn't like it, and drops them awkwardly to his side.

Is he nervous?

"Things aren't going so well between Respect and Rain. Something's going to happen, and I don't think you should have any part of it."

To think I need his help from a snooty-ass, arrogant clan member. He is wasting his time. "I'm not part of anything." I move to leave.

"Hey, girl."

I twist on him. "My name is Scream." He is trying to get me

in trouble. If Tobias saw me talking to him when obviously something is going on between the clans, I would get trampled.

His lip twists disgustingly, "Do you actually expect me to call you that?"

There's the clan arrogance I am speaking of. They think they are better than me. It is an attitude I've been met with too many times by Tobias' friends. Tobias isn't here, and I won't take it. Let him hit me if he wants. Tobias will return the favor tenfold.

"Don't talk to me; you won't have to call me anything."

A slight smirk twitches his lip, "I didn't think you'd be like this."

"Like what?"

"Defensive? I'm trying to help."

"You're trying to get me in trouble. Tobias won't like you talking to me."

His dark brows knit angrily, "Like I give a rat's ass what he likes. The guy's a prick."

I'd smile if I wasn't worried. "What do you want, Rain Member?"

"To keep you safe."

Ironically, he uses such a word, and it's the only word I associate with him. "Why?"

"Because I believe in you."

"In me? For what?"

"You're gonna save us."

I cackle. "I am? I think you got the wrong girl," I step toward the exit.

"You don't remember?"

I could keep walking, stay ignorant and keep trying to survive. But it's not enough anymore, is it? Surviving isn't how I keep Charles safe and happy.

"I don't remember," I admit.

Light eagerly comes to me, standing before me, "Then I'm right about you. Join my clan. Let us protect you from Tobias. We can help you remember."

I flick my eyes over his face. His black skin is smooth, situated on a gorgeous face with bright blue eyes like the sky. I see why he has his nickname. Light suits him. I think about taking his hand, joining his clan, and becoming like Drop. I can't imagine the happiness of having everything I ever wanted.

"Who am I?" I ask him. If I'm gonna 'save' him, he must know my name.

"I'm sorry," he murmurs. But what is he sorry for? Does he know and won't tell me? Or can't?

Light leans in, closer than I've ever allowed anyone, yet I don't back away. I want to know what he has to say. And, plus, he smells really good. "I know people who want to help. They believe in you too. You're the ember to the flames. You're what we need to restart our fight."

"Scream."

I jump at my name, finding Charles in the doorway. He's nervous, hesitant as he eyes Light. "You okay?"

"Yeah," I force out, stepping around Light to grab Charles' hand. "You ready?" I look back at Light. He wants to reach out for me, but I move Charles out the door, ignoring the feel of his eyes on the back of my head.

He's got the wrong person. I'm at the 'bottom of the cesspool'. I'm no one's *ember*.

16

Drama Queen

Charles and I spend the afternoon in the Wasteland. He climbs vast piles of trash and stands high as if a king. Charles no longer complains about the bumpy, rocky areas or the questionable liquid that soaks his flip-flops. He is adapting well. So much better than I had. I hope I had something to do with it. I'm proud, I guess. He laughs from his high position, then jumps down next to me, grinning. I pursue him, going faster with my long legs and aggravating him. I find laughter on my tongue more and more, and I love it. Laughing feels so good; I never want to stop.

Light comes into my mind throughout our fun, ruining the few peaceful moments.

Charles unwittingly made me feel ashamed of my name.

Light knowingly humiliated me.

"Do you think I'm gonna call you that?"

It is just a name, I tell myself. A meaningless thing, really. What is significant about a name? It doesn't define who I am. But how can I be proud of who I am if I have a sign above my head that says, 'weak'?

Ember. He called me an 'ember to the flames'. It's not a bad name even if it is misplaced.

Light said he believed I could save him. But save him from what? He lived comfortably in a clan. What was wrong in his world that he didn't like? So much so, that he needed saving from?

Does it matter? He believes in me.

My cheeks heat up and I press my hands against them so Charles doesn't notice.

I wait for the sun to lower before we head to the showers. I hate waking up in the middle of the night because of our smell. We could start to save so we can have things like soap and towels. With a home, we can store these items. I can have possessions that won't be nicked.

We get to the front of the line to trade our trinkets for tickets. There are people crowded at the gate, and it isn't until I get close enough that I find out what's going on. The guards are being thorough this time. I look at Charles. "You aren't hiding anything, are you?"

He shakes his head. I don't like his response. "Charles?" He keeps his eyes off me. "Put it in the basket." He twists his head so he won't meet my eyes. "Put it in the basket."

"I found it. It's mine," he grumbles.

Gripping his arm, I place my lips against his ear. "They will hurt you. You don't take from here. Everything belongs to Coal."

"They won't want it," he fights stubbornly.

My hands pat his shirt, panicked. "Where is it?"

"It's nothing." Charles pouts, pulling away. "It's not a big deal."

"Big or small, they don't care. It's theirs. Not yours." I curse under my breath. They are right in front of us, checking over someone else. He has shoes on, so he is obviously in some clan. They pass over him quickly.

When they get to Charles, my heart speeds up. If they are going to hurt him, I don't know what I am going to do. I immediately locate their weapons. I could slam my foot in one guy's gut, grab his gun, run to the next guy and use his body as a shield if the other chooses to shoot. Charles could slip out without anyone noticing.

I'd be killed.

My chaotic thoughts black out when the guards step next to me. They didn't find it. Whatever Charles had taken, he was safe. My breath releases.

"If today ain't my lucky day," the man from the left laughs. My gaze flicks to him. I hadn't noticed before, and now I wish I had attacked.

Prod, a prick with a beer gut. He isn't a teacher, but he's old like them. He wears leather cowboy boots with a big belt. He hooks his thumbs in his waist, emphasizing the belt buckle at the center, a buck with immense antlers. Big pit stains color his white button-down.

Prod approaches chewing tobacco, eyeing me with a wicked smirk. He spits at my feet, and a bit dribbles on his lip. I roll my lip in disgust.

Prod was the first man to become my enemy. Like every other kid, I woke on the bus, and he was there with his electric taser, poking kids to move. My first scar was a black two-prong design on my thigh.

"Now don't go giving me that look, darlin'. Just look at ya. Hooyee," he hollers, his men laughing beside him. "She's a perty thang, ain't she?"

I say and do nothing. Charles is in front of me, walking through the fence. He keeps glancing back as he hands over his basket. I smile in reassurance. I don't even let the jests bother me. But the heat creeping into my cheeks doesn't go unnoticed. I don't want Charles to hear any of these horrible things.

"She a wild girl too," Prod chuckles, slapping his leg. "She was a-bitin' and clawin'. You remember our fun, sweet girl?" His friends are cracking up, their eyes filling with that ghastly expression of interest.

Prod sobers suddenly, pointing at me with false fear, "Oh, look out now, she's gettin' angry. Alrighty boys, pat her down." His two guards come and grab me tight, their hands going in places they didn't go for Charles. "Get her good, boys. We don't want her keeping her stash somewheres," he cackles at that. Their hands go up further between my legs.

Charles' eyes widen, and I see his body seize. I shake my head slightly to get his attention. Thankfully a guard pushes him through.

The molestation lasts only a minute. Prod tips his hat, "You tell ol' Tobias I want to visit. He keeps turnin' me down, I might just show up when I'm good an' ready. Wild horses need a good handler, you understand me?" He slaps my butt, and I shove away, but it only makes him laugh, "See, fellas, now if she were mine, that wouldn't happen."

I give my basket, ignoring any other words that come out of his foul mouth. He'll get his one day. I'll make sure of it.

I head out, searching for Charles. He's gone to Zack's where we always meet up at. I run there. It's not a long distance, a little less than a mile. I find him sitting at one of the tables staring down at it.

The more days that pass, the more I see this contemplating expression on his face. I hate it. It's a face of experience.

I'm so stupid.

Raising a kid in hell, he's going to know hell. I can't stop him from learning. I can't stop him from understanding. But how can I teach him these things? I don't want him to change any more than he has to.

I sit down and wait until he voices what's bothering him. "Why do they call you Scream?"

I close my eyes when I hear Tobias' voice. It triggers early memories of the first few days of bedlam.

I went with Tobias because he promised protection. What I didn't know at the time was the cost of it.

"Scream for me."

I am embarrassed by my name. I hated it simply because Tobias gave it to me, but now I can't stand the thought of it. Tears itch at the back of my eyes, and I look away, refusing to catch his gaze until I pull back the tension in my throat and swallow. "It's a joke. Tobias likes irony." It's the best excuse I could come up with. I am determined now to find myself a new name. One that won't disgust anyone. One Charles could call me with pride.

He called me an 'ember to the flames.'

"Tobias is the leader of Respect," he reports. "He's partners with Coal. In trouble with Rain."

I watch him with concern. He's learning on his own, things that I don't tell him, things that shouldn't be important, but in reality, they are.

"He's a really bad guy."

I force a laugh agreeing with him.

"Are you his girlfriend?"

I scoff, "What do you know about girlfriends?"

"I hear things."

"Rumors," I scoff. "I thought you were smarter than to believe rumors."

"Hey, I am smart!" Charles quiets, and I can see the wheels in his head spinning.

I had hoped to steer him away from this conversation, but he's determined to talk about something I want to avoid.

"Why do you talk to him?"

I bite my lip, trying to come up with some reasonable answer. It's like making shit appear like rainbows. "You know how Mine tried to turn you into one of them? They beat you, told you things, and thought you had to listen."

"You saved me."

"I didn't have anyone to save me."

His brows crease, and his eyes flicker across the ground. He picks at the wood of the table, trying to find answers to the numerous questions while simultaneously being incapable of asking. I pray he doesn't.

"I don't like your name."

I take him up on the offer. "What would you like to call me then?"

"I don't know," he chews on his thought. "Fast? Mean?"

I smack his hand.

"You don't remember anything?"

"I don't even have dreams."

"No one else has that problem. Everyone remembers out there."

I search his face. Is this another rumor? He seems to believe it. Can I believe it? If they were kidnapped, it would mean I was too. And it would prove that I have family outside the walls. A few weeks ago, I couldn't care what anyone remembered. I couldn't see outside my own survival. But now, what if it's like pieces of a puzzle. All I need to do is put them together, and my memories will flood back in like magic.

"What do they remember?"

"Faces. People that took them. Some were taken on the way home from school. Others were in foster care, and no one cared when they got lost."

"What's foster care?"

"It's where you go when you don't have parents."

His words are contradictory, "But you said everyone has parents."

"Well," he stutters, trying to cover up his mistake, "They do, but some parents die. Or sometimes they can't take care of their kids, so they give them up."

I thought I'd have someone out there waiting for me. What if I don't? What if I'm really all alone?

'Your parents are dead,' Tobias said.

Charles hurries to assure me, "But if you don't, it's okay. You can live with me." He grips my arm, pulling me out of my head space. "You can live with me."

I give a fake smile to ease his worry. It's stupid that I'm grieving for parents that might not exist. I had made them up in my head, and now they're dead before I can even put a face to them.

Charles pulls out a little ball and throws it on the ground, only to have it bounce back into his hands.

"That's what you took?" I reproach, "Do you know how dangerous that was?"

"Everything's dangerous. Where we sleep is dangerous."

"What would have happened if you got caught?" I holler.

He shrugs, "I wasn't, though."

"Charles-"

"Relax, Scream." I cringe at the sound of that horrid name. "It's not a big deal. Maybe that's what we could call you. Drama Queen."

I snatch the ball out of his hand and run, laughing as he struggles to catch up.

17

Basement

I reach out in the darkness and wrap my finger around Charles' little hand. It's the middle of the night, and I'm plagued by nightmares. I dreamed we were taken to Auction. I could hear my name called over the intercom, but when I got up, Charles was in front of me. I ran after him, ran after the bus but no matter how hard I tried, I wasn't fast enough. It went over a cliff into a fiery hell.

I wipe the wetness from my face. I don't want Charles to ever see me cry.

I grab the shovel off the wall, jumping into the pit. We've dug about three feet so far. We've broken a couple shovels. The deeper we go, the harder the ground becomes. Water helps, but it is challenging to get a bucket of water here without spilling it. And, of course, we need to keep some of it to wash our faces and hands.

I dig for an hour, exhausted by the time the sky lightens. I'm beginning to think there is no end to the wall. I sit and stare at it.

If there is more to the world, then someone built this wall. Did they build it for us? For evil kids?

Movement, a shadow on the rooftop above me, gets me to my feet. I tilt my head back, searching for what I saw. I know someone was there. Were they watching me? Watching us? For weeks I've been feeling like I'm being followed. Most times I think it's Ruler, but if Tobias knew I was over here, he would have chained me to his bedpost by now.

I want to call out, to force them to show themselves, but whoever they are, they're gone.

I nudge Charles awake. I want to shower before school. I've sweat buckets too early because of the heat.

It's Reaping Day. As the months have gone on, and my understanding has gotten clearer, today is more terrifying than any other. Anyone is capable of being called to Auction, and no one is safe. Not me and especially not Charles.

"Can't we stay home?" Charles wonders as we leave the bathroom.

I wring my hair, and droplets of water sink into the sand, "Snatchers will come for you." I was able to buy new clothes for the first time since I've been here. Though they are a little big, they're fresh and don't smell.

"The Sky kids?"

"The ones dressed up like ninjas. They take kids the teachers don't like and bring them to Auction. They only come out one day a month."

"Today?"

I smile a fake smile, "Today."

"Scream," Tobias is walking toward me briskly. Hammer, Ruler, and Kevin are on his heels.

"What do you want?"

Tobias doesn't say anything as he snatches my hand. I dig

my feet into the ground, "Let go of me!"

He doesn't falter, yanking me along even as I twist like a kitten stuck in a ball of string. Hammer latches onto my other arm and I kick at the ground, but he continues stomping toward his house.

Charles is following, yelling, trying to grab for me, but Ruler pushes him to the ground, kicking at him.

My resolve changes. It's not about freeing me. It's about helping Charles. Instead of tugging away from Tobias and Hammer, I slam my heel on Hammer's foot and he screeches like a girl, his hold slipping. I dive into Tobias, knocking him to the ground. Now free, I hop up and run to Ruler, swinging my arm and slamming into the side of his head. He goes down with a curse, rolling into a ball. I pick up Charles from the ground, ready to run.

The familiar sound of a cocking gun stops me. I turn toward Tobias, and he stands with the barrel pointed at me. "Get in the house."

I stand firm.

He wouldn't shoot me. He 'loves' me too much.

Then his barrel shifts, just an inch- "Alright!" I give in. "Charles, get to class."

"But–"

I look back at him, and he shuts his mouth. I give Charles a side hug before pushing him along. Tobias puts his gun back in his pants as he approaches and grabs me by the bicep, "Why do you have to make everything so hard?"

I don't move nearly as fast as he tries to move me. "I'm gonna be late for school."

"You aren't going to school."

"But I'll get in trouble."

He cackles, "No, baby. You won't." He pushes me up the stairs to his building, and I burst into the living room.

I'm not done fighting, "Why aren't I going to school?"

"Don't ask me stupid shit. Get down to the basement."

The basement.

I struggle to speak, quickly trying to come up with excuses or promises, anything to keep me from going down there. I lick my lips, nausea swelling in my stomach. "But…I haven't done anything wrong."

Tobias steps up to me, "I doubt that." He stomps by me to the kitchen.

I stare at the front door.

I could run. I've always been a fast runner. But Tobias can stretch out his hand and snag me from any part of the campus. I'd rather not be a mouse for him to pounce on.

Kevin walks in. For a moment, I think about pleading with him. If he could help me, together we could defeat Tobias.

It's worth a chance. Isn't it?

But Kevin lowers his eyes and passes by me without a word. I don't blame him. He and I are the same, trapped in the orbit of an asteroid.

Hammer (slightly limping and glaring at me) and Ruler enter but Ruler stops at the doorway. The side of his face is red, and no doubt my hit will add to the bruises. He wants me to try to escape. I can see it in his eyes. He even steps to the side and leans against the wall, the door open, the light shining in.

I won't give him the satisfaction.

With haste, I swing around and go to the basement. But my speed dies as I stand at the edge of the stairs. It goes down into darkness, like a pathway to hell.

"Come on," Tobias whispered as he held my hand, "You'll be safe

down here."

"Think she's scared?" Tobias asks Ruler as they watch me. He drinks a soda, humored by my lack of movement.

"At least she remembers something," Ruler snickers.

Tobias tosses the empty can in the sink, "I'm impossible to forget."

Determined now, I go down the stairs like it doesn't feel like fire eating at my skin.

The lights flicker on, but there are only a few bulbs, and shadows linger on the walls. It's made of stone, with wooden beams. Old furniture stacks against the wall. Baby cribs and small toddler beds are broken into pieces, and a mattress lays on the floor.

"She's not gonna help anyone." Tobias bragged, standing above me. My body hurt too much to speak or move, and I lay half asleep on a small mattress.

"How do you know?" a foreign voice questioned.

"She doesn't remember."

"Are you sure?"

"I'll make sure she never does." A touch on my forehead made me shiver. "Shhh," Tobias mocked.

"It would be easier just to get rid of her."

"True, but where's the fun in that?"

I swallowed the bile. Dozens of words in the beginning, and I blocked them all out. Anything connected to this basement, to Tobias, had to be deleted from my mind. And yet now, it's at the forefront of my memory, replaying like the rules on the intercom.

I turn as Tobias comes down the stairs. He has a smile on his face, enjoying my fear. I keep space between us, backing up till I bump against the furniture.

"You said you didn't want me to remember. But when you asked if I had, you seemed hopeful. Why?"

Tobias ignores me, walking casually about. My fingers slide across a broken piece of a chair.

"You threaten me with Auction, but then you risk your reputation to keep me out of it. You say you save me every day, yet you abuse me in the same sentence. Nothing you do makes any sense!"

"I'm an enigma," he grins.

All the things I could call him, an enigma is not one of them. Tobias unhooks the whip from his belt.

I could be compliant. It might save me a little bit of the beating he has in store. But it won't stop it. And if it won't stop it, why should I listen? I usually don't go looking for a fight. But what if I could win? I've been getting stronger. I watch people fight, learning how to be better. What if I manage to beat him, best him, and I can get out? It will be similar to knocking down those walls. What if, by defeating him, I can escape this place?

I wrap my hand around a piece of wood, holding it out in front of me.

"There you go, being dumb again," Tobias tosses the whip on the steps. "Let's see what you got." He pulls his shirt above his head. Tattoos like his arms decorate his pectorals and abs. He stretches his neck, extending his arms. "You are getting better, I will admit. You're a fast runner. A quick thinker. You're good with the knife tricks and the bluffing. But you will never be able to beat me. Do you know why?"

My heart rate is escalating.

"Because I don't care if I hurt you. You still care. Not about me, but you still think you're good and kind. Scream, you're here because you aren't any of those things. You just can't remember."

"That's bullshit. I know I was taken."

"Oh, you do? From who?"

I clench my teeth, unable to answer. "You were taken too, weren't you?"

He open-mouth laughs as if it is the funniest thing he's ever heard. But it's fake. I know Tobias better than I know myself. It's a show he's putting on. And it's then I notice the camera in the corner. Even down here in hell, we are being watched.

Is it all a show?

He jumps at me, and I flinch. He cackles, backing up. "Come on, Scream. Are you that scared of me? There are worse people here than me, baby."

"No, Tobias. There isn't."

He grins maliciously, "Well, maybe not."

18

Believe

A door shuts and the vibration wakes me. Footsteps pat down the stairwell, slow and cautious. My breath comes in short pants. Dizziness clouds the ability to move and all I can think is that Tobias is returning.

Does he think I can survive another round?

The world is blurry, and the light makes it hard to identify shadows, but the fast-approaching evil makes me struggle against the pain.

A hand touches mine.

I don't want to die. I want to get out of here. I want to go home.

Tears drip off my cheeks and fall into the chasm of my bruised lips, "Please."

The chains lose their hold, and my body falls with gravity. It's agonizing. My body doesn't want to bend, not after hours spent hung from the ceiling. Someone holds me; their warmth would be welcoming if I had a friend. I settle on the cold floor, and though I want to shy away from it, I stretch out with relief. My torn muscles and wounds relax.

It's over. I've made it.

When a blanket falls over me, I open my eyes.

My fingers grace the fabric with complexity. Is this kindness?

Kevin lays out beside me, smiling a soft, reassuring smile. His hand brushes hair from my face, his thumb gently wiping the tears as they continuously pour from my eyes. His brows knit upon my sadness, and he shakes his head, holding up a hand. It is a silent gesture explaining that his intentions are pure.

He doesn't understand. I'm glad he's here. When Kevin shows up, it means Tobias is letting me go.

"I know why you don't talk," I whisper though my throat is dry and coarse. "Tobias broke your voice. Didn't he?"

His eyes, brown and so easily read, soften, and the smile forced upon his lips fades away. Tears come to his eyes, and he moves closer. His body heat warms me like a hearth fire. He doesn't touch, knowing well how painful a touch would be. His hand instead wraps around mine. The only part of me not damaged. Our fingers curl around each other. Equally dirty.

Is this what it feels like to connect? To have someone understand you and know you? I always fault Charles for being incapable of grasping who I am and what I've become when the truth is, I don't want Charles to be like me. I want him to stay innocent and pure.

At the same time, he and I will never be equals.

But Kevin can be. We have the same pain and past, tormented by the same man.

"He won't break me," I promise. "He can break my body. He can shape me into anything he wants. But I will fight. I will not go quietly, and I will get out. And I will go home."

Kevin puts a finger over my lips, shaking his head. He swallows hard, his Adam's apple bobbing and his lips press and tremble. A tear falls off his nose, and he wipes his face against his t-shirt sleeve.

"I'll come back for you." His face crumbles in pain, shaking his head, and against his better judgment, he hugs me, burying his face against my neck.

I will never leave him. He'll come with Charles and me. We'll be a family on our own.

***

I'm lying in Kevin's bed. Its mattress is sunken, and the sheets have holes in them, but it's got Kevin's personality in it, and I love it. There is a nightstand with a clock and a broken lamp. There is a closet full of clothes in green, black, and brown colors. It has to be his preference. I've never seen Kevin in anything bright or happy.

There is a poster on the wall, but it's odd and unlike what I've seen before.

'Learn English,' it reads in big, bold letters. 'Classes every morning at 7 a.m.' Beneath it are Japanese symbols. I remember seeing them when we learned about Pearl Harbor. My first class at school was a lesson about war and death. At the bottom, it says, 'Anyone speaking another language will be arrested.'

Kevin walks in with a plate of food. He smiles when he sees me awake. He sits it on the table and mouths the word, "Okay?"

"I'm okay." I look at the poster again, "What is that for?"

Kevin twists his face in awkwardness and holds up his hands, reminding me he can only communicate with sign language.

I giggle, "Sorry."

I eat in silence, staring out the window. Kevin has black curtains, but he opened them for me, allowing me to peer out. It shows the school in the distance. It's raining, and though it's the middle of the day, it's dark.

"You need to get stronger."

I hear Tobias's voice mixed with the sound of his punches.

"If I die, you have to take care of yourself. Do you understand me, Scream? You have to kill!"

Tobias thinks he's saving me. He believes in his claims so passionately. Perhaps it's vanity. He doesn't see himself as a villain. He thinks he's a hero. He's teaching me to be strong. Tough love, they would call it. Beat me senseless, so I learn. Is he that messed up? Is that what this place did to him?

Kevin sits on the bed with a sigh. He's been caring for me the last couple of days as I heal. When I woke up the second time, I tried to leave, but with a soft touch of his hand, I was reassured I was safe. He even assured me Charles was okay, so I allowed my body and my mind a reprieve.

Tobias doesn't seem to mind our friendship. Probably because he's a mute. I bet there are dozens of things he could tell me if only I understood his hand signs.

But there are always 'yes' and 'no' questions.

"Kevin," I whisper, unsure how the house echoes. "Do you know if there is a way out?"

He looks at me and then at the door.

"No. I mean, out of the school."

He snickers and shakes his head.

I chew my lip. "If I ask you something, will you tell me the truth?"

Kevin sits up and grabs my hand. He takes my pinkie and

wraps it around his.

"We're friends, right?"

He nods vehemently.

"I feel that way with you, too. You've always been nice to me. Do you know why I'm here?"

The emotions slowly drain out of his face. His hands slip from mine. He nods.

"Does it have to do with Memory?"

He rubs his bald head and nods again.

"Does Tobias believe in Memory?"

I don't know why I ask it. Why does it seem to matter? There is no reason for a monster to be a monster; it is just who they are. Yet still, I'm searching for justification.

He shakes his head, and I deflate, disappointed.

"Do you?" I wonder lightly.

Kevin peeks at the corner of the ceiling. The camera blinks in greeting. I tense upon noticing it. I never would have thought there would be cameras in the bedroom.

Kevin grabs a shirt from the drawer and goes to the camera. He tosses it up till it hooks, blocking the lens.

Rule 7: Do Not Block the Cameras

He puts a finger to his lips and stands beside the odd English poster. He has the corner in between his fingers and stares at me. I'm so eager to know what he's doing. The pain is momentarily forgotten, and I sit up, gripping the blanket.

Kevin lifts the paper up and reveals a different poster.

In bold white letters, in the chaos of graffiti, reads the words, 'Memory Lives.'

It's like the tags on the walls of the school. The ones that the teachers painted over, hoping no one saw. It's a dangerous thing to possess, but Kevin hoards it with care.

A door shuts, and Kevin drops the poster, running to snag the shirt off the camera. "Kevin!" He's out the door, closing it behind him, leaving me blown apart.

Kevin's a part of the rebellion. He has the answers that I'm searching for. He knows who I am. Others know who I am.

Does Tobias? Is that why he treats me so badly?

Kevin pops in the room and waves his hand.

"I'm going?"

He nods viciously, whipping the blankets off me. I'm in his pajamas, but he grabs my arm and gently but aggressively pushes me out the door. I struggle with the stairs. My body is stiff from lying in bed for days. The house is empty, and I go out the front door without a snarky comment.

As I step out into the rain, I look up at the sky allowing the raindrops to fall on my face. The touch is cold but welcoming. I can't help but smile. I've been released from hell and I made it out alive. No matter how dark it seems out here, it's refreshing. I'm seeing my world for the first time with hope in it. Out there, where I only took notice of the violence, of the hate and deception, where I only paid attention to the pain and loss; now has bits of light, bits of happiness, bits of excitement. There is a rebellion stirring, one that wants to be unleashed, waiting for an 'ember' to start a spark.

And I could be that ember.

19

New Name

I observe Charles as he stands in line for dinner. He keeps his head down. A bruise covers the side of his face, and a cut on his arm has closed and scabbed already. But he's here. He's made it through the Reaping and three days without me. I'm proud, yet a little disappointed. I want him to need me like I need him.

I am horribly selfish.

I think back to the first time I saw him. He had a newly shaved head, little specks of blood on his scalp, clothes that didn't fit, and bruises all over. In only a couple weeks, he appears more grown up and not like a nine-year-old. His skin is darker, his hair is growing back, and a look in his eyes shouldn't be there.

He is no longer so brand new. My heart aches for the life he's missing out on.

I'm knocked over by his hug. I'm laughing as he's crying. I pick him up and sit us on the stools. I tire quickly, having been resting for so long.

"What did he do to you?" Charles questions, looking me

over.

I'm thankful my clothes are bulky, hiding every bruise and welt. "It doesn't matter. I'm back now."

His tiny hand fists against his thigh, "I hate that guy. He's terrible. I want...I want to hurt him."

Me too.

"Don't think of him. He's too dangerous."

"He shouldn't get away with it."

"But he does. No one will stand against him."

"We could."

I roll my eyes, "What could we do?"

He shrugs, picking at his food. His brows knit, but all I see is an angry kitten. He's adorable.

"So, how was the weekend? Did you manage to get back to the hideout?"

"No. I stayed outside the Respect building waiting for you."

I sigh, resting my elbows on the table. He's so stubborn. "Charles," I begin. "If I'm not around you have to take care of yourself."

"There's something you should know, Scream," Charles mumbles, refusing to meet my eyes.

I cringe at the name. I really hate it now.

I want to get him out of his mood so I shake his leg with a smile, "Like what? You get a girlfriend while I was away?"

He clenches his teeth, keeping his eyes away from me.

My smile drifts, "What's going on?"

"There were pictures."

"Pictures? Of what?"

"You."

I sit up with a stiff back, confused but frightened nonetheless.

"Tobias," Charles murmurs. "He put up pictures on the walls

of the school."

"Of me?"

He nods, and a tear drips out of his eye, but he rubs it away quickly. "Chained up in the basement."

I struggle to breathe as I hold my head in my hands. I never wanted Charles to see me like that but to know not only him, but the whole school humiliates me far worse than anything Tobias has done. Why does he go so far? What does he want? What have I done to make him hate me so much?

I have to get away from him, and the only way to do that is to escape.

I stand up, "Let's go get more shovels. We're digging us out of here."

"Scream."

I flip my eyes over, and Light stands before me. His body is tense, and he's shaking with his hands into fists at his side. "Are you okay?" he asks, barely capable of getting it through his tight-knit lips.

I nod, speechless. Every time I see him, he springs feelings inside of me I haven't felt before. My stomach rumbles as if I'm hungry, my face blushes instantly upon eye contact, and I become self-aware of my appearance, and I fidget, tucking hair behind my ear, straightening my poise. Tobias has never made me feel like that. If it is a bad, evil thing, Tobias would have caused it, right?

"Hi!" Charles interrupts, "I'm Charles," he holds out his hand.

The interruption breaks Light out of his fury. He awkwardly takes Charles' hand, smiling, "Light."

"You're huge. Like football player huge. Do you play?"

"No. I never did."

"You'd be unstoppable."

I smile at Charles before turning my eyes back up at Light. His gaze softens, the tension slipping out of his body. "Thanks," he murmurs, "I should get going." Though he says it, he doesn't move, staring at me. There's more he wants to say but doesn't. Instead, Light leans over, a hand on my shoulder, a touch I don't shy from. "After school tomorrow. Run here."

I look at him, as close as his, the blue of his eyes feels like staring at a full moon, "What are you going to do?"

"It's time to end this."

I know what he means without any further information. His clan is going after Tobias but what I don't think he realizes is how powerful Tobias is. I'm afraid Light will get hurt even though I'd love to see Tobias destroyed. "Tobias is too strong. You can't win."

"Hail is going to fight him. One on one," Light straightens proudly. He has a smile on his face now, and confidence rallies in him.

My heart leaps. Hail is the best fighter in this school. Tobias doesn't stand a chance.

Will he die? Oh, wouldn't that be something?

If Tobias no longer ruled my world, if I was free and fearless, how would I be? I could walk with a head held high and a back straighter than ever thought possible. I'd be happy.

I catch Light's eyes. Could he understand? Could he know what this would mean for me?

I almost feel the need to thank him. He's going to do what I can't. But I have nothing to give. I have no way to pay him back for fighting for my freedom.

I offer the only part of me I can give that wouldn't ruin my pride. "Ember."

He questions with knitted brows.

"I thought that would make a cool name."

Light grins. A gorgeous, full blown smile that lights up his face and transforms him. How can one person be so attractive?

"It suits you."

I watch him walk away, taking with him the excitement he instilled in me. My smile slowly fades when the stupid blinding wall finally drops to reveal reality.

Tobias will never die. This is his world we live in. And Light isn't doing this for me.

"Ember, huh?" Charles questions. "I guess that will do. I still like Crazy better."

20

The Fight

Charles and I dug in the sand until our bodies were too sore. I gave up sooner than he did, but in my defense, I'm still recovering from torture. The rain had set us back a few inches, but it made the ground softer. We were able to go two more feet.

Still no end to the wall.

There is excitement in me as we start the day. Though I don't believe anyone could take down Tobias, the fact people are willing to try assure me I'm not wrong in my assessment of Tobias. He's evil, and I must get away from him before he twists me into someone unkind. He's the only person that makes me think bad things.

I took a shower and put on the new clothes I bought in the market. They were expensive and took everything I had, but it was worth it. A bright blue shirt and jeans. I look like a Rain Clan Member. I want everyone to know where my support lies.

More importantly, I want them to notice I am not wearing

the black ribbon around my arm.

There are conversations about the fight as I walk to class. They are all as excited as I am, but they simply want to watch a good fight. They aren't as invested in it as I am. Kids stop chatting in their groups and gawk at me. This time, I keep my head up, proud of myself. Today, I gain my freedom.

When I enter the classroom, it gets quiet. I take my seat with a hammering heart.

Tobias pops in at the entrance.

Does he know he's going to die today? Can I be the one to tell him?

If this my last chance to talk to him, I'd ask him why? Why did he hate me? What did I do to him for to hurt me and constantly belittle me? I was a lost little girl in this world and he took it upon himself to keep me buried with my head in the sand. Who knows what kind of person I could have become if he hadn't strapped chains to wrists and kept me down.

He looks around wildly, passing over me with indifference, before his eyes land on someone. He comes in swiftly, weaving between desks and pushing a kid out of his way.

In the back of the classroom, Hail leans against the wall. He has his hands in his pockets and his foot propped up behind him. He flicks his dark hair out of his face, watching Tobias with a barely-there-at-all expression of annoyance.

Looking at Hail now, I never would think he was a fighter. Unlike Tobias, who is riddled with tattoos and random piercings, Hail is unsullied. Where Tobias' muscles are defined and sharp with a dark tan, Hail is pasty in color and drained. He's terribly melancholy and focuses on Tobias with tired eyes.

Rain Members come between them, stopping Tobias from approaching any closer.

THE FIGHT

"Don't do this," Tobias urges, and it surprises the class. There are whispers of disbelief. Even Light adjusts his position in confusion.

Hail is apathetic at best. "You've given me no choice."

Is Tobias scared? I crack a smile, silent laughter building, threatening to burst.

Oh, to watch him gravel! It is thrilling.

"Want to run, pussy?" Cloud taunts. His boys laugh with him.

Tobias ignores them. "Five years, Johnny."

My brows knit with a sudden wave of pity that bulldozes my thoughts. They've been here that long? Tobias isn't fussing because he's scared, but the prospect of fighting a friend must be a tragic circumstance.

Maybe it would be possible if Tobias still possessed a heart.

"This job was given to me. I'm doing my job!"

What job? Am I the job?

Hail pushes himself off the wall, cutting into the line of Rain. "Don't do this here. We've talked enough. You've taken it too far, Tobias." His enormous hand raises and points right at me. "You had that girl strung up like a gutted pig when you know what she means. You've lost it, brother."

My face burns from humiliation. The eyes that turn to me feel like pins pricking my skin.

"It's Drop," Tobias continues, putting a finger in Hail's face, "She's gotten into your head. She's turned you against me. All for a fucking girl. You'll betray me—"

Hail leans back against the wall, his hands returning to his pockets. He shakes his head, so full of disappointment it's visible. "You've got it backward, bro. I'm not the betrayer here."

"You'll die," Tobias whispers so softly it is almost a plea. I want to see Tobias' face. To look in his eyes and see what it is he is feeling.

"We'll see."

* * *

When the school bell rings, I want to run. But I can't. In fact, I don't move. Today could be my liberation. The death of one man could help end all wicked thoughts and awful feelings.

I won't know fear.

I will be innocent again as long as Tobias dies.

But if he doesn't, if he survives, the chains he placed on me will last forever. I cannot be free if he is alive. I cannot run if he follows, and I cannot let go if he tightens his hold.

Footsteps drag across the floor, and I watch Hail approach me. I sit still, afraid I'll spook him like a drifting ghost.

Hail stops in front of me. "Scream."

I swallow.

"I know who you are."

My eyes widen, and my heart pounds in my chest.

"After this is over, I will make up for the wrongs done to you. I should have... I'll explain everything soon. We lost hope, and it wasn't fair to you. But I'll make it right. I promise."

He's out the door before I can find words. I sit back, blinking, crying, his words repeating in my head.

Who am I? Why do I matter?

I try to block it out, to say I don't care and shove it down, like I shove down everything, every question, every nagging, confusing piece of information that slips into my ears. But I can't.

THE FIGHT

Who am I? Why do I matter?

Charles breaks into my thoughts and pulls at my arm. He's as eager as anyone to see a fight.

Out in the schoolyard, in front of the steps, a circle forms around the two opposing forces. Tobias is on the right, and Respect members stand in a semi-circle, keeping the crowd back.

Hail is on the left, with dozens of Rain members brewing like a lightning storm behind him. His head is high above the crowds. Light is standing with Drop, her face a blank canvas.

Hundreds of kids try to see over each other. I step up on the balustrade of the stairs to see down into the fight. Charles wiggles in front of me, and I keep my hands on his shoulders to keep him from falling. And for emotional support.

As I continue to notice who has shown up for this battle, dark shadows appear on the rooftops. It seems even Sky is interested in the final score.

Tobias refuses the first swing. My teeth ground with agitation. How can he suddenly act so well-tempered? How can he act like a martyr when he's the dictator? Does he want pity? Does he want us to see the 'soft' side so we won't hate him so much? So many freaking questions, and all I want to do is scream at him.

Act like the lunatic who whips me till I puke. Act like that merciless demon who strung me up 'like a gutted pig'!

Hail's giant fist slams down right in his jaw, and Tobias falls to the ground, spitting blood from his split lip.

Charles yanks my hand, "Why don't his friends help?"

"School law permits one-on-one. No weapons, no tricks, and no help."

"Or what?"

"Expulsion."

"You mean, they get to leave?"

"I think they die, Charles. We just don't see it."

Tobias gets back on his feet. He dodges another fist and slams his shoulder into Hail's stomach, knocking them both down with Tobias on top. After that, I can't tell what is going on. The pace is too fast, a bunch of different fists being swung, legs being kicked, and dust smoking the area.

Yet it is Tobias who is on his feet. He's panting. Blood pours from his face, and his eye is swollen. He looks down at Hail, who attempts to get up. "Don't," Tobias orders.

Hail stands again, and for a moment, he sways on his feet with his eyes on Tobias and catches his breath. His shirt is ripped, and he yanks off the rest, throwing the cloth to the side. Tobias mumbles something but takes off his own as well.

They rush at each other again, fists punching the air in wild throws, kicks missing bodies, elbows, and knees, finding their targets more than not in this bare-all free-for-all.

Why won't you just die, Tobias? Why can't you give up?

Tobias stands again.

Every punch on Hail's body is like a stab to my chest. I can see my hope dwindling away. Hail made a promise he could not keep. I want to stop the fight. I want to save him the way he's trying to save me. My legs don't move.

Hail gets to his knees and tries unsteadily to continue to his feet. His clan hollers his name in support, but there is no more for him to give. He pants heavily, and blood is everywhere.

Tobias comes to him and puts a hand on his shoulder to whisper something into his ear. The crowd is so deathly quiet, but I haven't a hope to hear what he said. Hail shakes his head, and Tobias looks down at him with disbelief in his eyes and steps away.

The giant gets himself to his feet, and Rain cries with jubilation.

But I only pay attention to Tobias' face. The honest emotion he's exposing is rare, and no one else seems to see it.

He's sad.

The next round is the last. They roll for a minute before they end up on their knees with Tobias behind Hail, wrapping his sizable muscular arm around his neck and gripping Hail's hair to keep him still. Hail fights it but his strength is depleting, and then his arms fall to his side. Tobias whispers something again. This time Hail nods. Hail stares ahead at Light, at Cloud, at Drop.

He smiles once.

Tobias repositions his arms, his hands gripping Hail's head. There is a sudden scream from somewhere, sharp but short. Tobias snaps Hail's neck. The sound is like a giant tree breaking under the duress of a storm. The crowd rolls in shock, and for a few seconds, there's no movement, no sound. We observe as Tobias lays down the body of his friend cautiously and with great care.

I'm numb.

All at once, a reaction. The Respect and Coal roar with excitement, and they jump around Tobias, slapping him on the back and shoulders, slapping each other as they act like monkeys.

Rain remains silent and motionless. Drop and Light seem determined not to grieve as they watch the celebration of the death of their friend. It must seem unreal.

Light believed in Hail so much.

I observe Tobias with unblinking eyes. He stands at Hail's

head, bleeding and beaten, staring down at him. All the arrogance and pride he usually wears on his sleeve is gone. A different person stands there now and I don't know who it is.

The crowd quiets down when Drop steps forward. She is so strong. No tears burn her eyes. I wish I knew how not to cry. I wipe my face pathetically.

She wants to say something, something meaningful, or spiteful. I can see it in her stiff shoulders and her heated glare but what words can undo what's done? "The disagreement between our clans is over," her lip trembles and she swallows. "Not one Rain member will raise revenge against Respect, and if Respect comes at us," she pauses, gathering her strength. "Then it will be their downfall." Drop lowers her voice, "Take your victory lap, Tobias."

Tobias flips his eyes up to her, and all the emotions that had been vacant resurface and direct at her. His hands curl into fists. I nearly step out, afraid he's going to hit her. But he turns away and shoves through the crowd. No one knows what to make of it as they watch him stomp off. The crowd disperses, unhappy with the show.

Light leads a few men, taking Hail's body up on their shoulders and following her out. I watch the procession, wishing I could tell him I'm sorry. He seemed so sure yesterday today everything would be better.

I tug on Charles' hand, and we hurry off campus.

"What do you think he said?" Charles wonders. "Tobias whispered something important."

21

Family

Everywhere we go, there is talk of the fight. An hour ago, the battle had ended, and false rumors were already flying off adolescent lips. Hail had fought and died valiantly, yet they sit there and mock a dead human being. Do they even care about the people mourning the teen's death?

I mourn him, and I didn't even know him.

'I know who you are.'

I mourn the information he kept from me. Why couldn't he come right out and say it instead of waiting?

'I'll make it right. I promise.'

It's stupid of me to feel betrayed by a dead man. I put so much hope into something I knew wouldn't work out. Why am I so stupid?

Why do I hope at all?

I flee to the Wastelands. Charles wants to play, practicing his punching and kicking at the motionless waste piles. I provide fake smiles, barely hearing him at all. I'm stuck in a downward spiral of 'what if.'

What if Tobias had died today?

I want to be free of Tobias so severely I wanted him to die. Not figuratively, and not for some lame dream, but I actually wanted him to cease existing. That's not something a good person wishes for.

But I'm not good, am I?

I don't like my thoughts. I force out a conversation starter. "Tell me about out there."

Charles glances up at me and thinks, "I've told you a bunch already."

Yet it's still my favorite topic. "What do you do for fun?"

His eyes get really bright. "There's this game called, soccer. It's like kick-the-can—

"I know what soccer is."

"My mom coaches my team."

My brows knit at the way he said it. Like it is the present and not the past. Like if he got out, all of it would be waiting for him.

What's waiting for me?

"Anything else?"

He shrugs, "We go to the movies." Charles sits on his knees, "If you forgot everything, how do you know what soccer is? Or how did you know to brush your hair and take a shower?"

I never thought about that. "It was natural. Instinctual. It's weird. I know words. I know the meanings. I knew how to talk when I got here. I knew how to read, but my existence…what made me, me. Who I was is gone."

"I don't get it."

"Well, cars, for instance. I know what they are. But I don't know if I've ever been one. Cows and ducks and bears, I know what they are, but have I touched one? Seen one? I don't know."

"That's weird. Did you know how to fight, too?"

"No, but it does come easy. I think I was a runner."

"Yeah, you're super fast."

I bow my head, "You know, I never really imagined who I was until you came along."

"Really?"

"I didn't know I was missing anything. I thought I was normal. I thought this world was normal."

"But it's not."

"I know that now. But for a while, I was sure the other side of the walls was the edge of the planet."

"What about history class?"

"It was in the past. It was all gone now. Everything but here."

"Where'd the kids come from?"

I look away, "You're gonna laugh at me."

"No, I promise."

Embarrassed, I admit, "I thought they were being saved."

He snorts, "From what?"

"Fire? I don't know."

Charles bows his head, trying to hide his laugh, but I know what he's doing, and I flick his ear.

"Owe!"

"Tobias told me there was fire out there. The kids that left were burned to death. That's why I never thought about escaping. It was a great lie. If nothing else, Tobias is a fantastic liar." I force my attention on the ground beneath my hands. I hate myself for believing anything he said. From the first day, he had me ensnared in his world. He took advantage of me in every possible way he could.

"What are boys like? Out there?"

"Why? Cause you got a crush on that Light guy?"

I don't look at him.

A crush. This feeling inside, is that what it's called?

Charles drops a candle in the basket, "My dad is really nice. He smiles and jokes. He has a big laugh that makes you laugh."

"Does he hit you?"

Charles reels, "No!" he shrieks. "I just said he's really nice."

A person can be nice and still beat you.

"He picks me up and puts me on his shoulders. He plays soccer with me whenever he comes home. He makes my little brother fly, and he loves it. I get jealous sometimes, but I want him to have fun with dad too. My sister doesn't talk to my dad, though. All she likes to do is slam doors and scream. She gets so angry over the stupidest things."

Sadness is creeping inside him. I can see it like the clouds rolling in with a storm.

"I was so close to my home that day. I could see my house. If I had only been faster, or stronger, or smarter—"

"Charles," I crawl over to him, wrapping him in a tight hug.

"It wasn't fair. I'm a good kid. I knew about strangers. You don't go in the car with anyone, whether they offer candy or say they need help. But this kid was sitting on the side of the road with a busted knee. She was crying so I thought I could help make her feel better."

"She was taken too?"

"No," he murmurs into my arm. "She sat there and watched."

How could she sit there and do nothing?

"I bet your family is looking for you."

"I know," he sniffs, resting more comfortably in my lap. "But

I'm too far."

"What do you mean?"

"The bus drove for hours. I don't think I'm in Texas. It took longer to get here than it does to go to my grandma's."

There isn't a way to assure him. Life outside the walls is like an alien race. How long would a family wait to get back their kid? How far would they travel? How hard would they fight?

Is anyone fighting for me?

I hum a tuneless tune, staring out across the wastelands. The walls tower above, ever so present. Whoever built them made it impossible for anyone to climb over. Even standing on top of the school, the highest building here, it doesn't reach the top of the walls.

"What are you singing?" Charles wonders.

Singing is just singing. "Nothing."

"It sounds familiar."

"It's the only sound I know."

"Maybe it's from your home."

The idea never came to mind, but I really like that. "Maybe."

22

Grief

In the morning, Charles and I head for breakfast. We pass by Mine members beating up someone, and though Charles wants to help, I grip his arm, turn him away, and force him to keep walking.

It ruins the morning. Charles sits at the table, picking at his food and refusing to talk to me. I paid extra for some bacon, but it didn't even make him smile. I'm not going to apologize, but I hate that he's mad at me.

"How," he begins, "are we going to create a clan if we don't help people?"

I humored the clan idea because of boredom and hatred for Tobias, but did I have any intention of actually starting a clan? *Not at all.*

"There were a dozen Mine members. I can't fight them all."

"I can help."

I give him a skeptical look.

"What? I know how to fight."

"No," I snicker. "You don't."

Charles goes back to sulking quietly.

His happiness is important to me, but building a clan sounds impossible. I don't know where to start. Charles thinks all we have to do is help someone, but the risk of helping is what stops me. Percentage-wise, I haven't won half of the fights I've been in, and I'm still recovering from the one I lost.

He has high expectations, and I'm afraid he'll be disappointed. I want to win for him, so, therefore, I will only fight the battles I can.

My name echoes through the building. Ruler hollers from the front as if he's too afraid to step inside, but I know he simply lacks manners.

"Now what?" I grumble, standing as kids looks at me, whispering. My face heats up from embarrassment.

Charles grips my arm, stopping me.

"It will be alright," the words come out easy even if I don't know if it will actually be alright.

He doesn't let me go, coming with me to glare little daggers.

Ruler's tongue plays with his lip piercing as we approach, "Now, you rebellious little girl, where have you been?"

Charles spouts out, "The third Rat building."

"I've been to all the buildings," he replies icily.

I nudge Charles to shut up. "You must have missed us."

"You better not have been near Coal. Tobias warned you already."

"I thought I was rebellious."

Ruler chuckles, "That's why I've always liked you. Even getting strung up like a gutted pig," he uses Hail's analogy to annoy me. "You still got balls." He flings his arm around my shoulder. "Now tell your little shadow to get lost."

I glance at Charles who stands like a pissed-off kitten.

"Charles, go on. Eat your breakfast." He doesn't move, but Ruler tugs me along.

"What's going on?" I ask, thoroughly bothered he still has his arm on me.

"Tobias wants you."

"I haven't done anything."

He laughs again, "Oh, you're not in trouble. Relax."

"I'd relax better if you'd get off me."

Ruler pulls me tighter against him, "Don't get cocky."

If Tobias doesn't want to punish me, then why send a search team?

Inside the Respect building are more members sitting around. There is a somber atmosphere that makes me nervous.

Ruler announces my presence, "I found her!"

Tara scoffs at the sight of me, "Her? He wants her?" She storms out of the place.

A few of the boys laugh, "Jealous much?"

Jealous of what?

Ruler pushes me, "Go. I'm sure you know the room."

I catch Kevin's eyes. I'm happy to finally see him. I want to talk to him about the poster, but the swelling around his eyes tells me this isn't a good time. He's been crying. He smiles tightly, fake and insecure. He turns away from me.

With a deep breath and a straight back, I climb the stained carpeted stairs and down the hallway. The walls are made of light-colored wood with a single light in the middle, leaving the hall's beginning and end in darkness. Each step I take feels like stepping in slime.

"Wake up. It's time for your first day of school."

The last time I was in Tobias' room was my first week here. He had taken me there after he had gotten done beating me, and he dropped me on his bed like a carcass that's carved up for dinner.

I turn the knob and slowly peek in.

The room is barely lit, with a single lamp in the corner. The TV sits on top of the dresser with a dark screen. A large queen-sized bed is in the middle with gray and blue bed sheets. Nothing else is decorated, and that's how I remember it.

Plain ugly walls.

Tobias stands in front of the window. It's funny because the only thing outside his window is the big indestructible wall.

I don't close the door, and I don't move any closer.

As the minutes tick by, I can no longer be quiet, "Tobias. Why were you looking for me?"

He snaps his head around as if he hadn't heard me come in. His brows knit, "Where were you?"

"I was in a Rat house."

"Ruler can usually find you. He's been searching since last night."

I shrug, "He must have stepped right over us."

"Us?"

"Charles and I."

"You and that kid," he shakes his head, turning his attention back to the window. "It doesn't matter."

"Tobias, what?" I ask, annoyed.

Without turning to me, his hand reaches out.

I think about leaving, about running, but I don't want another bruise. I step closer, looking at his hand as if it's laced with poison, and I uneasily touch it. Tobias pulls me close, and then just like that, he's hugging me.

I attempt to push him away, thinking he's going to kiss me, but he only hugs me, and my hands are in the air, not knowing what to do with themselves. It takes several seconds before I rest them at my sides. An odd position in this lonely hug. His hand squeezes my hair, and I cringe, thinking he's going to grip it in an extreme fist, but even that thought subsides with time.

I don't like this, and I glance around, hoping for something to smack him with.

"I needed you last night. After what happened," he whispers into my neck.

What is this? What is he doing? Is he grieving?

Tobias doesn't know what Hail meant to me. How could he? Hail was going to help me escape this monster, and now I am in a one-sided hug with it.

I'm the one who's grieving.

"You didn't have to kill him," I nip, swallowing the bile in my throat.

"It was either him or me. And I can't die yet."

"Why not?" The question is much harsher than I intended it to be and yet genuine.

Tobias releases me and goes to the bed. He sits with his head in his hands. He doesn't speak for a while, and I glance toward the door, wondering if I could slip out.

"We created the clans together," he begins. "We took on the teachers, and rescued Memory from the Snatchers. For four years, we were inseparable. It sounds so unreal now."

Tobias reveals so much in such a little sentence. Pieces to my ever-building puzzle.

More so than ever, I'm assured Tobias knows who I am. He has taken me into his control for a purpose. Perhaps to stop a rebellion. He leads me by the leash, keeping me where he wants me. He reveals only enough to keep me wanting more but never sedated.

Without a memory, I focused more on building myself and learning how to survive than anything else. I didn't worry about the world outside the walls or wonder how I came here. Trying to find food and staying off anyone's radar was more critical.

But Charles opened so many doors, and now none of them will close.

All the memories I have, I need to go through with them with a fine-toothed comb and see if I'm missing anything else.

"What split you up?"

Tobias stares up at me.

It's shocking how innocent and young he appears right here. The bruises on his face are bright and big. He's never looked so fragile.

His gaze alters, and he snaps to his feet. "The Grounding," he states with bitterness. His attention is back on the wall.

"What's that?"

"A year ago when everything went to shit. Memory left us, and then Drop comes in with her Peace Campaign and ruins any hope for another attempt."

Another attempt at what?

Tobias never gave me direct answers before. I look around the room, searching for the red eye, and to my astonishment, there isn't one. A place in this world that isn't watched.

What does Tobias do for the Teachers to allow him a place with no cameras?

"Violence is necessary. Memory is proof that the teachers aren't going to be taken down easily."

'Taken down.' He's fighting in the rebellion. He has to be. It's a giant piece of the puzzle that I need to help solve why my life has become this horror film.

"Tobias. Do you believe in Memory?" The questions comes to my lips again because I know it's important even if I don't know what it really means. But if he believes in Memory, then maybe, he believes I have something to do with her.

He cackles a dry, harsh sound. He doesn't see me, his eyes are on an item on the dresser. It's a small snow globe, but I can't see what's inside it. Tobias touches his face, his fingers grazing the scar on his face. "No. Not anymore."

I don't want to believe him. I'm still searching for why he's become the monster he is. I'm still hoping for an excuse.

Tobias shifts his head to me. His scar isn't visible from this angle, nor is the constant smirk it causes. He almost looks normal.

"You still don't remember anything, do you? Do you even know your name?"

"Do you?" I whisper with sudden hope. "Tell me."

Tobias moves towards me, and my head raises to keep his eyes on mine. There is humor in his gaze now, an expression I've seen before when he wants to play a fucked mind game. He rests his hands on my arms, "I know many things."

He disappoints me, and I hang my head. I know what he wants. I've always known what he wants.

What if I could do it? Just once? I could close my eyes and pretend to be somewhere else while he does whatever he wants.

"Maybe if," he steps even closer, our legs touching, our bodies touching. If I gave in, he'd tell me everything. If I surrendered to him, I'd have a name, I'd have memories, I'd have a past to build myself on.

Fingertips on my chin raise my resistant head. "Love me," he whispers, leaning down to tempt my lips.

I shove him, stumbling backward and tripping on the bed. I

roll over it and keep the bed between us. "Love you?" Horrified by the thought, I can't help the disgust in my voice, "Love you?"

I thought all he wanted was physical, but he wants love? How could he ask for something I don't possess-that I could never possess?

"I can get you out of here, Scream."

"That's not my name." Tears spill down my cheeks. I don't care if he could get me out. I don't care if he has my name. He'll never get anything from me. I'll die in this place before I give in to him.

He laughs, "How do you know?"

"I may not remember my real one, but I've created my own. I'm not yours to name, Tobias. I will never be yours."

The humor dies quickly, and the doors open to the devil. Tobias grits his teeth, the muscles in his cheeks flexing. The scar on his face shifts, "I've owned you since the moment you came here. I'm the reason you've lasted so long. Me!" He steps forward, but the bed separates us. "I'm so sick of you," he growls as he walks toward the door. "I killed my best friend for you," he shuts it and presses the lock. "And I want you to thank me."

I crouch down, the adrenaline pulsing through, shaking my hands. He blocks my only exit, but that doesn't mean I'm trapped. I'll bulldoze through him like a bullet. He flinches, and I step back. He laughs as if this is a game.

Tobias moves for me, and I try to dodge, twisting, but he snags my wrist, spinning me. His other arm loops around my back, pushing me against him. I smack anywhere I can, his face, his shoulders, his arms, but he knows how to keep his eyes away from my fingers, his throat protected from my elbow. He knows all my tricks. He slams me against the wall, and air pushes from my lungs. I cough as he grabs my hands and pins them above my head. His face comes straight at me, and I squeeze my lips tight so he can't touch them. I close my eyes, panting wildly through my nose, constantly pulling against his hands, but he's too strong.

I'll find a way out. It's not over.

His hold loosens. I snap my eyes open as he backs away, "I didn't ask you here for this."

I'm so confused I can't move. Why be merciful now after months of torture? "Then why?" I shout, surprising even myself.

What else is there? Love? What the hell does this boy know of love? What do I know of love?

"Just go."

Tears blur my vision. I run out, wishing to keep my sobs within me. He makes me hate everything about myself. He manipulates me into thinking I've somehow hurt *him*.

I slam the door to the house with a hand against my lips and rush down the steps. A person grabs me, and I yank away from it, spinning around to find Tara sneering at me.

"Oh, stop it," she bites, pulling me away from the other members of Respect and around the corner. She shoves me back, and I hit the wall.

"What is your problem?" I cry, "Why do you hate me?"

"You don't fucking get it, do you?"

"No! I don't get it."

Tara and Tobias are a team of confusion and manipulation. They work to ruin me. Why does Tobias want me to love him? Why does Tara believe I'm like her? Why can't either of them leave me alone? "Explain it to me, please!"

"I like your suffering. It makes me happy."

I stutter, shocked by her boldness. "You're a bitch."

"I may be. But at least I know my name." She steps closer to me, "You are a lie. Everything about you is a lie. Why can't they see that?" she whispers, and her eyes flick over me, searching for the answer. Cruelty splashes on her face, "You don't know anything. You are a fucking shell."

"Rather be a shell than a stuffed slut."

She mocks me with a "oohh.. good one." Tara struts away to the exit of the alley. I watch her leave, despising her as profoundly as Tobias. Her head leans to the side, "I'd be careful. Think of how angry Tobias will get when he finds out you have a little crush?"

How does she know what I feel for Light? I barely know what I feel for him.

The bell rings, reminding me it's still a school day. This day is gonna be a long one. I want a nap, exhausted by Tobias' emotional insanity. Instead, I head to the school. Charles is sitting on the steps, searching the expanse of the schoolyard and when he sees me, his eyes brighten, and he waves.

Then all the happiness fades out of his face, and I stop. He's looking behind me.

23

Cloud

Cloud stands in front of me.

I'm only a few feet from the school's main entrance, and if I can get inside, Cloud and his friends won't be able to hurt me. I turn to go, but a Rain member blocks my path.

I face Cloud. Within the group, Light blends into the colors of his clan with a bowed head, too ashamed to look me in the eye.

With confidence I don't have, I force out, "Drop told you not to mess with Tobias."

Cloud steps forward. He lifts his hand, and I flinch. He smiles, reaching forward to flick a piece of my hair out of my face. I smack his hand, and he steps back in surrender.

"I'm not messing with Tobias. I'm messing with you."

"Same shit, dumbass."

Cloud touches my arm, "I don't see the black sash," I smack his hand away again. "Technically, you're not a part of any clan. Which makes you fair game," he chuckles, glancing at his entourage for encouragement.

"That's not how he'll see it."

My heart thumps. I look at Light. I don't know why I'm hoping he'll come to my rescue. I thought that he liked me or perhaps it was all my imagination. He keeps his eyes on the ground, telling me he can't stop it.

Or won't.

"You know," Cloud murmurs, "If you took a shower and dressed like the other girls, you'd be kinda hot."

I watch him as he circles me, "Thanks for the advice."

Rule 13: Do Not Harm or Lie to a Teacher or a Clan Member

I have to get out. Somehow, someway, I have to get out of this mess. If I go left, I'll end up in Coal Territory. My only option is to go right and somehow get to the Respect Building. But the only way I'll get there is if I can run faster than any of them. Cloud has already won a race before when he caught me in the bleachers weeks ago.

I crouch. If fighting is my last resort, I will fight with everything I have.

Cloud throws a punch, and I dive beneath it, punching him in the knee. He curses and limps in a circle. I smile when he glares at me. "For that alone, I could get you to put up for Auction. Tobias may have protected you this month, but the one great thing about the Reaping, it always comes back around. Kinda like Christmas."

What did Tobias do? Why is he always trying to save me while hurting me?

Cloud punches me, and I drop to the floor, holding my face. I blink forcefully to clear the black spots in my vision. The pain radiates down my jaw and into my ear.

Fucking Tobias. Even when he's not here, he's screwing me up.

I struggle to get back to my feet, but I can't stay down, not from a single hit. Charles is watching. I shake my head, standing, swaying, and holding my hands up. A crowd is forming around us now, and I can hear their obnoxious cheering. These kids really need manners.

Light steps forward, "That's enough," he snatches Cloud's arm. "No more."

Cloud pulls his arm out, facing him, "You're gonna protect her? After Tobias got ten of our members taken in the Reaping?"

He did what? How much power does he have? So much he can get people taken to Auction. So much he can live without being watched.

"Exactly," Light replies, "Look what he can do. Tobias has the teachers behind him, so why do you keep messing with him?"

"Because he's fucking fake. Like you. And when I expose him and you, the teachers are gonna favor ME!" Cloud hits Light in the chin, but it barely affects him. Light returns with a punch of his own, slamming into Cloud's cheek, and the kid staggers backward, falling to the ground. He holds his face, shocked that his friend actually hit him.

It felt good to watch, and I don't hide my smile. As Charles pointed out, Light has a bodybuilder's strength and knows how to use it.

I definitely have a crush now.

"What's going on?" Drop's voice interrupts, and though it sounds like an angel, I don't know what she'll do with me. I hit Cloud, and if she wants to punish me, there's no getting out of it.

The group parts for her, and she comes up from behind Light, a hand resting delicately on his shoulder. Her eyes find me and widen, "Oh."

Dressed in dark clothes to represent her state of mourning, she has on tight pants and a beautiful silk blouse. Her hair curls around her, but it's easy to see her sadness, her eyes bloodshot as she examines me. She walks up, and I can only stare at each graceful movement, each hypnotic step.

"You think this is revenge?" Drop shouts over the noise, ending all conversations. "One meaningless girl equals the weight of Hail's loss? Our clans have a truce."

Cloud gets to his feet, blood dripping from his nose. He rubs it with the back of his hand, "Hail's dead because of her. We lost Mist, Flood, River. How are you gonna stick up for her?"

Drop is not intimidated by him, "I'm not. I hate her too. But I won't let you jeopardize anyone from this clan. Do you understand me, Cloud?"

"It's bullshit. You're weak. Maybe it's time we find someone that can handle a bit of violence."

Drop doesn't speak. She glances at me, and I shrink under her scrutiny. I'm at her mercy, and I know it. She has a power I'll never possess. "You want to know what's bullshit?" Drop inquires. "How you got those scratches on your face. What did you tell me? A cat? You're the one that attacked Tobias' people, aren't you?"

Cloud steps up to her, but Light and several others don't like it. They come to her aid, and even his close friends grab his arms to hold him back. Cloud snaps out of it and points a finger in her face, "You ain't gonna last without Hail."

"You're out, Cloud. Or should I call you Milton?"

Cloud or Milton cackles nervously, "I'm out? You can't kick

me out."

Drop gives him no more attention stepping around him. She walks by me as if she doesn't even see me. Rain trickles behind her like fog and even as Cloud tries to grab hold of someone, his hand slips through.

Light puts a hand on my back, "Stay away from him," he warns as he guides me onto school property.

"Light," I want to apologize for Hail and to thank him for sticking up for me, but words freeze in my throat as I meet his gaze. He's so close to me I can make out the long lashes of his eyelids. He smiles, softly, reassuringly, just enough for me to notice his lips.

"Light," Drop calls.

He bows his head and steps back, "We'll talk later," he promises before he rushes after her.

"Scream!" Charles runs into me, gripping me around the waist, his face buried in my chest. "I mean Ember." His voice muffles against me as he holds back his tears.

I hug him while I observe Milton/Cloud. He doesn't seem to know what to do. He looks around wildly. He's alone, standing in front of the fence of the school. He appears lost as if he was dropped in the middle of a battlefield, and he has no idea whose side he's on.

I would pity him if I didn't find it funny.

24

Pieces

I watch from the building's edge, spying on Charles playing with boys his age. He's swinging on the monkey bars, lifting himself up to stand on top and jumping down, like he always loves to do in the Wastelands. He's so strong. He's gotten bigger too. Despite the dirt, bruises, and cuts, Charles plays with other kids with no hatred or fear. At any moment, he could be broadsided by a Mine member or a group of clan members wanting to hurt others. None of that matters. He is a child here.

I want to see him grow up. I want to witness what it's like growing up. I want his hair to grow back. I want him to get taller than me. I want him to get strong and tough and one day protect me from everyone. He'll be my shield. He'll grow into someone good. He won't hurt anyone. He'll stay perfect.

But for that to happen, I'll have to make sacrifices, and I'll have to protect him in ways I might not like.

When I wave, he happily runs to me. It's the weekend. It's been a week since the Reaping took place. I never noticed the difference before, the feeling that reflects in everyone after the

Reaping. Kids are nicer for a time. They follow the rules with vigor. There is less violence while at the same time a larger presence of fear.

Perhaps at this moment, the kids and I are more alike than ever before. Like me, they realize every day is a struggle to survive. I focused so much on getting through it daily. I didn't know how limited that made me. I can't focus on just today. I need to be prepared for tomorrow or a week from now. I need to set up Charles for success.

I want him to become a clan leader if we cannot escape. It's the only position that's safe enough, perhaps not to keep him out of Auction, but it will stop him from being picked on and beaten.

It's a backup plan, but even a backup plan needs preparation. And who has the power to make him a leader?

Tobias.

We head to the Wastelands and play a game Charles invented. We play around to waste time and afterward we head to the cafe for dinner. It's the same gruel as every other day, but we got a piece of chicken and mac and cheese with some tickets.

On the way home, I hand him a piece of chocolate. It cost a bunch of tickets, but chocolate is my weakness. He shakes his head. Not because he doesn't want it but because he wants me to have it. I love him even more.

"Do you believe in God?" he asks. I frown at him, and he quickly explains. "There is a group of kids that stay under the bleachers. There's a hole in the fence, and they get in there and pray. I sat and watched them while you were away. They seem happy, praying. Like it takes all the bad stuff away." He stares up at the sky.

"Do you?"

He shrugs, "I don't know. If there is, why make us suffer? We're kids. We're good. Shouldn't He help us?"

"Maybe it's more like the cameras." I point to one as we pass, the red dot like an alien orb in the dark, "Maybe He can watch, but He can't do anything about it." I look at the sky, wondering if I could spot God hanging out. "I don't know much about God. I know a lot of people killed for it. And were killed for it. Seems stupid to me."

"Why do you think those kids keep praying? If it's not doing anything."

"It's something to believe in."

"What do you believe in?"

I look at him.

It reminded me of Light when he told me he believed in me. It was the weirdest thing, and I didn't quite understand it. But as I observe Charles, I get the feeling Light felt. "You."

He cracks a smile. He doesn't say anything for a time before he grabs my hand, "I want to show you something."

"The guards are gonna switch out in ten minutes."

"We'll be quick," he assures. Reluctantly, I follow him. Charles takes me down Dark Alley and in between the two apartment buildings. The fading day is all the light applied, and it's only a matter of time before this area is completely dark. I run my hands along the wall covered in graffiti. Frayed pieces of paper clip my fingertips, some crack beneath my touch after years of being out in the weather.

Zack's poster, 'Spread the Love.' repeats like a toilet paper roll. On the other side of the wall, Rain's mantra: 'Wash away and start anew,' is written with clouds and raindrops.

Charles removes something from his pocket and a small light beams on the ground. "Where'd you get a flashlight?"

"I bought it in the market."

The darkness helps hide me. A flashlight is like a siren.

I chew my last piece of chocolate, "What are we doing?"

I notice the Boundary poster, 'Shield and Stone, bound as one.' They sound like an army. Too bad they are useless at protecting anyone around here.

Charles lifts a poster and shines his light on the wall. At first, I don't know what I'm looking at, but Charles directs the light over it. Mixed into another drawing are disguised letters, written in black marker, 'Join the Anarchy.' I kneel down in the dirt to get closer, inspecting it as if it's a rare jewel. "What's it mean?"

"Memory wrote it."

I look at him. "It's the rebellion." Though it's not a question, he nods, "Do you know who Memory was?"

"She was the leader of Rain before the Grounding."

His words are so confident like he read them in history class.

I imagine Memory sitting right where I am as she wrote this dangerous message. She must have been so brave. I'm consumed by her, and I've never met her.

Charles glances over his shoulder. The movement is so obvious because it's something he's never done before. I peek around him, searching for what he's afraid of. Charles leans over and whispers, "They don't want me to tell you."

"Tell me what? Why?"

"They're scared. They think the teachers sent you here. They think you and Tobias are putting on a show."

"No, no-"

Charles puts a finger to his lips, afraid when my voice rises. He looks up at the corner of the building. The camera is far away, but it can still see. Can it hear us? Does it matter?

I put a hand over my mouth and ask, "I don't know anything."

"I keep telling them that, but they don't believe me."

Who are they?

Charles straightens, and with a sudden pep in his step, he hollers, "It looks like a wiener!" he laughs, pointing. "It's even got balls."

I quickly follow his cue, slapping a hand over his eyes, "Don't look."

"It's not like I don't see one every day," he wiggles out of my hold, "I am a boy."

"This is what you wanted to show me? If I wanted to see wieners, I'd go to the Coal Building."

My mind is racing, even as I chase him through the alley. The guards are already gone when we get to our hideout, but as we move, Boundary walks by. I pin Charles against the wall, using the darkness to hide us.

One of them stops to tie his shoe.

"Come on," I hiss under my breath, cursing his very existence.

How hard is it to tie a freaking shoe?

It makes me think, I've never had shoes, so I'm not quite too sure how hard it is.

Regardless, it shouldn't take this long.

The seconds count until the Boundary member is back on his feet, fixing the rifle over his shoulder before moving on. I snag Charles' hand, and we rush across the sand, diving into our home.

That was too close. How long until someone finds us?

"Let's try to find a different place to live."

"Why?" Charles clearly doesn't like the idea, but he's aware of the red dot in the corner as well as I am. If Tobias can sleep without it, are there other other parts of the world that don't have someone watching?

"I'm tired," I lay in the sand with my back to Charles, staring at the wall. I know he observes me, but I pretend to go to sleep. There's no point in talking when what I want to talk about, I can't say. Instead, I dive into memories, into moments that have stood out since I first could remember.

The bus.

The sight of the school.

Kids rushing toward me.

I fast forward through these terrifying events, trying to pinpoint conversations. The only problem with this is the feelings it brings. My body shakes from the fear.

The light of the basement.

The rough texture of handcuffs.

Tobias standing in front of me.

"What did Memory say to you?" Tobias growled as he dug his nails into my neck.

I snap open my eyes, panting, crying.

I curl into a tight ball, praying Charles isn't watching me anymore. I can't think of any of it. I don't want to.

I take a deep breath, forcing my thoughts onto positive things: Charles' playing the wastelands.

Breakfast in the morning with strawberries and bacon.

Chocolate.

'You're the ember to the flames,' Light whispers, 'You're what we need to restart our fight.'

'If I have her," Ash's bitter voice breaks in, 'the rebellion will be as good as dead.'

'You think you can steal from us because of who you are?'

All these little snippets are hints of who I am supposed to

be.

What if I already know how to escape and I can't remember it?

I sit up when another memory hits me.

'There's a war going on, sweet boy. There's always a war.'

Zack spoke to Charles but why do I get the feeling he was talking to me? Hinting at the rebellion?

Zack's always been nice to me. He's provided me with clothes and food, especially in those early days when I was so confused I wasn't taking care of myself. Why would he help me? Does it mean he's on my side? Shouldn't he be on the teacher's side if there is a war between the teachers and the students?

But Zack has always been different.

He's the only teacher that lives here. Or he's a prisoner too.

'Stay away from Zack,' Tobias warned.

What if Tobias is keeping me away from Zack because Zack knows who I am? It's completely something he would do.

Guess I'm going to disobey again.

25

Zack

In the morning, at breakfast, I leave Charles again. He doesn't like it, but with a stern look, he stays. I go across to the Spread building. Throughout the night, I thought of the questions I would ask Zack. I've been here for nearly four months, and I've never asked my name. But to be honest, I hadn't been focused on who I am. I didn't believe I was important enough to think about. But now, if who I am matters, I need to find myself again.

The kid at the entrance lets me in but stops me in the foyer. They make me take off my flip-flops and replace them with paper slippers. They squirt my hands with antibacterial soap and spray me with Lysol. I don't know if I should feel insulted or not. They point me down the hall, but I'm hesitant. Tobias had so much fear in his voice when he warned me to stay away. How could a monster be afraid of anything?

Unless Zack's a bigger monster.

I force myself to go down the hall.

The carpet is a plush red. There are antique oil paintings of naked women hung along the corridor which is disgustingly creepy. Candles on wall holders are attached to the flowery wallpaper. Wax drips down the wall like vines. It smells of lavender with a hint of bleach lying underneath. Each door we pass is closed with a number on it. Every step away from the front entrance increases my anxiety. I look back, and the kid kneels on the floor and sucks up any dirt I've brought in with a small handheld vacuum.

At the end of the hall, double doors open up, and I peek my head in. Dark red curtains hang along the wall, and bean bags and blankets make up different sitting areas. In the center are round tables sitting on the floor. Big tube-like things sit in the center with a cord attached. Zack lights a long incense stick and waves the vapors into his face, making his bracelets tinkle.

He smiles as he greets me, "Hey, my sweet girl."

I suppress the urge to cringe.

He waves his hand over, "Come in. Sit. I'm so happy to see you. Tsk," he reaches a hand to my cheek, "Always with the bruises." Zack pulls me to the velvet couch with his veiny hand on my arm. He sits with me, crossing his legs. He's dressed in a loose-fitting dress that hangs long on the arms with matching slippers. "So what's up, sugar bear? Why are you here?"

"Do you know my name?"

He digests my question and then pops up to his feet, "Are you hungry?"

I grab his arm, "Zack."

He swats at me, "What makes you think I know, darling?" He goes over to his desk, shuffling papers around as if he suddenly lost something. His bracelets jingling with each movement.

"Tobias knows."

"Well, Tobias is different from the rest of us, isn't he? I imagine he knows more than most. Tsk, where did I put that necklace? I saw this in the marketplace and thought you would love it. Jam-Jam!"

I stand up, "Do you know who I am?"

Zack stalls, examining me, "Do you?"

I shake my head.

Zack sighs with disappointment and sits in the chair, losing interest in whatever trinket he lost. "I don't know if you are an excellent liar or you actually don't know."

A door swings open, and Jam-Jam enters. I've seen him with Zack, one of his bodyguards that he calls a 'Special.' His dark eyes pass over me like I'm another relic in this odd room. He stands at Zack's desk, silent, waiting.

"Can you bring us some coffee? Make it sweet. Oh, a piece of chocolate for Scream. She loves chocolate." Jam-Jam bows and steps out.

Why does Zack know that about me? It's not something I've ever talked about.

"I'm not lying," I manage to reply. He's different here, in his rooms. He's taken off all his masks and is bare before me. I shouldn't be here, but now I don't know how to get out. Could I just leave? Would it be that easy? Somehow, I doubt it.

Perhaps I shouldn't have disobeyed Tobias this time.

Zack plays with a ring on his thin fingers. He studies me, his old eyes wrinkling at the edges. "Why are you here?"

"I thought you'd help me," I feel stupid for saying it.

"Haven't I? I believe I've helped you plenty. But when have you ever helped me?"

Why didn't I ever consider he'd want something in return for all his friendly gestures?

I'm a fool.

I look around. If I have to, I can smash Zack with the pole

on the table. He appears feeble enough that I don't worry about his strength. What I should concern myself with are his bodyguards. "What do you want?"

"What did Memory tell you?"

Once again, someone thinks I have something to do with Memory. It has to be true, then, doesn't it? Memory and I knew each other on the outside. Were we friends? Family? Did we go to the same school? Live near each other?

"I keep telling you, I don't remember."

"Well, I don't believe you anymore. So what shall we do about that?" He taps the desk, searching for an answer among the mess. "I might be able to help you remember," he says it casually, nonchalantly, as if the thought just came to him.

My stomach is in knots. It's the feeling I get when Tobias approaches me. The sweetness of his words barely cover the maliciousness inside him. I should go, run as fast as I can and bulldoze my way out, but if he doesn't know I've caught on, he might let me go. "What can you do?" I ask with a bit of false hope.

Zack smiles, "Plenty."

Jam-Jam walks in with a tray. A single cup of steaming coffee and a piece of chocolate. He sets it down on Zack's desk and stands back with his arms stiff at his side. "There's a phone call."

Zack hops up, his dress waving like a flag as he zooms over to the door. He spins at the last second, "Have a drink, and I'll be right back. Jam-Jam, will you keep her company?" Then he dives through the door and disappears.

My eyes flick to Jam-Jam. He meets my gaze with the emptiness of a painting. The tension is all one-sided, all my imagination or my intuition.

I take a step back. Could I make it out before Jam-Jam can reach me? He has long legs, a longer reach, and he's stronger. But I can't think of all the reasons I shouldn't try. I *have* to try.

Jam-Jam steps forward, and I reach for the long pipe on the table. His hand is on my wrist as if he knew exactly where I was going and moved before I did. I look back at him, and his face is close enough for me to finally see an emotion buried deep within it.

Fear.

"Go," Jam-Jam orders.

26

The Grounding

My nerves are raw as I run away from Zack's creepy house. When I find Charles. I can't think with my heart pounding and my blood pulsing. I'm pacing, shaking, trying to keep panic from developing. I have no idea how close I was to something terrible. Sometimes, I'm the stupidest person alive. No wonder Tobias has to take care of me. I'd be dead thirty times over if it wasn't for him.

Charles watches me, unsure of what to do or say, and I ignore every question he sends my way. I keep putting up a hand. I have to calm myself down. I don't know if I'm overreacting, but I can't get the disgust out of my stomach.

I drop against the wall and sit on the ground.

I'm safe. I'm okay.

Against my better judgment, I pull out the black ribbon from my pocket. I hate it and yet, every day I learn a little bit more and come to a disgusting theory that Tobias is protecting me, despite the terrible way he goes about it. He has his claws into influential people, and he can make things happen.

I wrap the sash around my arm. It's like a blanket on a cold night, and it helps calm me, but it's also embarrassing. It's a leash, keeping me out of danger because I'm too stupid to recognize when it's not safe.

As my mind begins to clear, I can focus. I smile at Charles. He squats in front of me, waiting. I hold a hand out, and he helps me to my feet. "Are you okay?"

"I think so. Did something idiotic. Don't ask." I demand fervently.

Why did Jam-Jam help me? I never would have imagined he'd betray his warden. Will he get in trouble?

"Why'd you go into Spread?" I notice the tint of blush on his cheeks.

I push him away, giggling, "I'm not joining."

He releases a breath of relief, "That's good."

"Let's just stay away from Zack for a while."

"Great idea."

The school bell rings, and we head to class. I keep my hands fisted at my side to hide the shaking. Charles helps by talking about something random, and I allow all my thoughts to focus on his voice. By the time I sit at my desk, I've relaxed enough that my heart is no longer in my throat.

I'm startled when a folded piece of paper lands on my desk. Awkwardly, I pull it open, *'Stay after class. Need to talk. Light.'* I stuff the paper in my pocket, sitting straight, trying to appear like I'm not a nervous wreck.

Class doesn't start fast enough while I think of everything he could want to speak to me about. Of course, the apparent gang-related stuff, but could there be another reason? Does he want to see me, as I want to see him? I bite my lip, and my stomach curls in nervousness. There is no way he likes me. Not when there is someone like Drop beside him.

But Drop was Hail's girlfriend, so I might stand a chance.

All through class, I'm trying to fix my hair and wipe the dirt from my face. I smell my armpits, relieved I showered yesterday.

The bell rings, and I am slow getting up, pretending to fix my pant leg, my shirt, then I proceed to search for something on the floor. I kneel, looking under the seat.

"What are you doing?" Light's bothered voice sounds. I flip my hair to look up at him. He holds out his hand, his eyes at the door, a nervous gesture before he rests his eyes on me.

I don't take his hand as I stand, "What do you want?"

Light drops his hand. He leans back against a desk and folds his arms across his chest, his eyes on the ground, avoiding me. "I wanted to apologize," he murmurs.

At first, I don't know what he's apologizing for, but his brows knit as he analyzes my face. The bruise I've gotten from Cloud is small but present nonetheless.

I'm speechless. It's the last thing I expected. If anything, I thought he would yell at me for getting in Cloud's way or for not wearing the black sash. Both were my fault, and Tobias would have no problem telling me that.

But he's not like Tobias.

"It's alright," I manage to get out awkwardly. "You didn't have a choice."

"But I did. I just got confused about who I was following."

The way he looks at me dissolves words. I swallow, sweating.

He's brows knit, "How could I let you get hurt?"

"Let me?" I cackle softly, thankful to be pulled out of my reverie. "You have zero control over what other people do and especially me. I'm not exactly avoiding confrontation."

A smile presses on his lips. Humor envelopes his face, and I struggle to keep the heat rising to my face as I agonize about how gorgeous he is.

Light reaches out, and I flinch back. He stops, waiting. I've never been touched by anyone other than Tobias. I'm curious to what it feels like. To what care feels like. His fingers rest on my jaw, his thumb brushing over my cheek.

It's everything I hoped it would be.

A warmth spreads through my body and I bow my head, fearful he might notice. His hand falls back at his side. It gets quiet after that, and I glance toward the door, afraid Tobias might walk in. Tara's warning replays in my head, telling me I must leave before Tobias finds us. If he learns I have feelings for Light, I have no doubt the next Reaping will take him away.

But I don't want to leave his presence yet. "I'm sorry, by the way," I say, "About Hail."

He nods, "Me too. I thought he was gonna win for sure. I still can't wrap my head around it. I mean, I was there, and I still don't know how he lost."

"Tobias is a fighter."

"Hail used to talk about him. They were friends once; did you know that?"

"Tobias said something. He said the Grounding split them up, but I don't know what that is." I sit on the desk, letting my legs swing. It's relaxing in his presence, and I'm unafraid. I feel normal for once.

Light uneasily shifts, "I was there. It was about a year ago. The Grounding is what the teachers called it. Like when parents punish their kids."

"What happened?"

Light approaches and sits on the desk beside me. He's so close I can smell his cologne. I take a deep breath and try to pass it off as a cough.

"There was talk about a rebellion for a long time. Carbon and Memory were the leaders and they got a bunch of kids together to take on the teachers. They set up an attack. And then..." he pauses, remembering the day with a heavy sadness. "Then they were all killed. Over a hundred kids were laid up in the middle of the schoolyard. A mass grave till a dump truck came and took them all away. I can still remember the smell. It's not something you forget."

"That's..."

That sounds worse than anything I've experienced so far. "So Memory is dead." I'm disappointed by that fact. There's so much hope in her, but it's empty hope. "Why does everyone think I have something to do with Memory if she's dead?"

Light watches me, "You may not remember, but has Tobias told you anything about what's going on?"

"No. He doesn't like questions. And I can't really tell when he's lying, so there's no point in asking."

Light snorts, "Piece of work, that guy."

"Yeah."

Light moves to the opposite desk, facing me. He leans his arms back on it, stretches; it flexes the muscles, a *hefty* amount of muscle. I flick my eyes to the ceiling, so I don't openly gawk.

"Memory's body was never found. There are those of us that believe she escaped, and she's trying to get us out."

The implication isn't lost to me. If Memory is trying to get them out, and I'm supposed to know her, than my job is what? To help? How can I help when I don't know who I am?

I jump off the desk, "I should go–"

He touches my arm, "Ember."

I'm not used to the name yet, but if it sounds as good as it does from Light's lips, I'll warm up to it in no time.

"If I can get it set up, would you meet a friend of mine?"

"For what?"

"I think he could help you."

"I still don't remember anything, so if he's looking for answers, I don't have them. I'm sorry." I don't want him to put his hope into me. I'm nothing. I'm no one of importance. I'm struggling worse than any of them to get out of here. It's stupid of him or anyone to think I can help.

"What if this person has answers for you?"

Light mentioned before there were people here that might know who I am, but so far, the ones that know who I am seem to want something from *me*, and I've got nothing I'm willing to give.

"Sure," I say, indifferent.

Light eagerly barrels on, reaching for my hand, "Come with me now."

There is an urgency to him that sinks into me, but I'm skittish. I trusted Tobias so quickly when I first got here, and look what's happened to me since? I trusted Hail, and he let me down. I trusted Zack, and I almost never saw the light of day again. Too often, I jump without searching for a place to land first. I can't take any more risks, not when I have Charles waiting for me.

"Please?" The desperation in his voice breaks me.

But I have to keep taking risks, so Charles doesn't have to.

"Scream," Tobias interrupts, standing in the doorway. His eyes are on me, sinking into me like a piece of hot coal on paper. His whip is in his hand, a tight, white-knuckled grip. Hammer is on his left and Ruler is on his right, looking over his shoulder with a satisfied grin. Kevin and Tara are in the back. His whole brigade is here.

I back up, putting as much space as I can between Light and me as I stumble on words, trying to defend myself, defend Light, but I don't know what to say.

Light steps around me, relieving me of responding as he announces, "I'm done, boss. Ain't no harm with conversation," he speaks civil, relaxed, and heads toward the door.

Tobias and Light stand inside the doorway, only a few feet apart. The tension between them is tangible, making it difficult to breathe. If they fought, would Light cave under Tobias like Hail had done?

Tobias points a finger in Light's face, "If you touched her…"

"She'd enjoy it. More than I can say for you, huh, boss?" Light glances at me and winks. He slaps a hand on Tobias' shoulder, "It wasn't her fault. Had a question about class. We good?"

Tobias clenches his teeth, the muscles in his cheeks flexing. He doesn't say anything, and I wonder if he's afraid. He nods once, and Light pats him on the back as he leaves. It's silent as Respect stands there, watching Light head down the hall. My whole body is shaking.

Tobias turns his devil eyes toward me.

27

No More

Tobias steps into the room.

I tread backward, putting as much space as I can between us. I'm reaching for a desk to keep it within my reach. It could be a weapon, but for now, it's a shield.

"Why was he talking to you? What did he tell you?"

"Nothing. We were just talking."

"Did you fuck him?"

"No!" my face heats, and I look away, "Can I go now?"

Tobias advances toward me, and I shove a desk in front of him, but he slaps it out of the way, and it crashes loudly to the floor. He grabs my arm, pushing me backward until my back hits the wall. I grip his wrist when he wraps his hand around my throat, squeezing with only a hint of what he can do. "Over and over, I tell you not to do something stupid, and you don't get it." He pulls out his butterfly knife, flips it open, and presses it against my cheek. "You are gonna join my clan. Be protected and be by my side—"

"Never."

I didn't mean to say it out loud. But I wouldn't take it back even if I could.

I put the black sash on my arm because of the protection I receive. But who or what is protecting me from Tobias? Out of all the monsters here, he is the most dangerous. If I can't be saved from him, why bother with the others?

For a moment, I thought I could surrender to him. I could feign love. I could pretend affection. I would use him to get what I want, to keep Charles safe. If there was nothing left of me as a result, then oh well. I'm not really whole to begin with. I'm an 'empty shell' like Tara called me.

Perhaps my pride is too great, and I'll regret this. But staring him in the face, there is no possible way I could give him what he wants.

The knife digs into my skin, and I keep my lips squeezed shut even as the pain intensifies. My silence is my defiance. No matter how hard he tries to get me to scream, I won't do it. I won't give him that satisfaction.

Kevin smacks his arm, finger spelling something in front of Tobias' face. Tobias doesn't look away from me, his brown eyes unreadable even inches from my own. I hope what he sees in mine is determination.

He will not be the ruler of my world.

Tobias pushes away. I press a hand on my cheek, pulling away with a spot of blood on my palm.

Tobias points the blade at me as he steps backward, "Let's see how long you last without my protection. You won't make it the weekend."

"I'm tougher than you think." Yet even as I say it, my heart begins to pound. I hadn't been prepared for him to cast me out. I didn't think he ever would.

"Since when? I broke you the first day you got here. I didn't even have to try."

His words only fortify my decision. I do not need him. I'll get better; I'll get stronger and faster and smarter. I'll learn the truth about this place and who I am. "I'll make it. I will always make it."

"I'll wait for the knock on my door when you're ready to come back. It won't take long to realize just how good you had it." He swings away, other members following, Ruler chuckling, and Kevin giving me a look of sympathy.

I rest my back against the wall, overwhelmed and relieved and reeling from the terror.

"Tsk, tsk, tsk," Tara leans against the door frame with her arms crossed.

I stand up straight, refusing to look weak in front of her. I won't let her make me question myself. What's done is done. I'm free. Unlike her, I managed to get away with respect for myself.

It takes too long for her to say whatever it is she wants to say. I gruff out, "What?" When she doesn't answer, I move for the door to get away from her.

Her mouth shifts into a condescending smile, along with a twinkle in her eye. She stops me from passing by her. She slides her fingers up my arm, pulling the black sash away and holding it up. The symbol of my life in her hands.

"You'll come back."

"Why the hell would I?"

She ignores me and disappears, leaving me by myself.

I look around the room, consumed by the fact I'm alone. Without the protection of Respect, the weight of my decision looms over me in the quiet. I never thought I'd care about what Tobias does for me, but now that it's gone, I'm afraid. I've never been on my own before. I blamed Tobias for everything that's ever happened to me. Now I'm responsible for my own safety and Charles'.

I rush out of school, constantly glancing over my shoulder as if the news of my departure from Tobias would make national headlines. I snag Charles, and we rush along, but I don't even know where to go. We can't get to our hideout for another four hours.

Charles gets annoyed with me. "Would you stop that? What's going on?"

With nowhere to go, I lead us to the Wastelands. Charles attempts to help clear my mind by being playful and silly. I pretend to let his tactics work, if only so he doesn't catch on that anything is wrong.

As the sun sets, we take the junk we collected, trade them for tickets, and then head to the cafe for dinner. It's a safe place despite Zack lurking on the side with his bodyguards with him. Jam-Jam stands as still as ever, but seeing him again, reminds me of the terror I saw in his eyes. There's a soul buried deep within him, and I can't imagine what Zack has done to him to keep it locked away so tightly.

Would Zack do the same to me?

I look away before Zack can notice.

"Why can't you tell me what's going on?" Charles probes.

I shift uncomfortably in my chair, shoving a scoop of mashed potatoes in my mouth, so I don't have to answer.

'You won't last the weekend,' Tobias said.

Despite it being a threat, it was also a warning and one I have no problem listening to. "We need to stay in our home for a couple days."

"Days?" Charles stresses in outrage. "You just said we need

to find a new place, and now you don't want to leave it?"

I get up and throw my plate in the trash, "Let's go to the market before it closes. We need supplies."

Charles crumbles and rushes to fill his mouth with food before throwing his plate away.

He wipes his mouth with the back of his hand, following. We are late to the market, and some kiosks are already closing. I pay double the price for a bushel of apples, a jar of peanuts, and two bottles of water. We have some snacks at the hideout, ones that don't spoil in the heat. But it wouldn't last us two full days unless we ration. I bought two new shovels. Might as well work as much as we can on the hole to keep us entertained.

Charles carries the shovels over his shoulder as we make it to the other side of campus. "I found out something new."

"What?"

"This place," he gestures around him, "It's a holding facility."

"For what?"

He rolls his eyes exasperatingly. "For kids, dummy. They bring us here until they can find buyers for us." He glances at my face and answers my silent question, "To buy us."

I appear unbothered by this 'rumor,' though I know there is some truth to it. Tobias hinted at it before.

It's not something I want Charles to think about so I continue to play dumb, "Why would anyone buy kids? That doesn't make any sense."

Charles stares at me. The gaze in his eyes I can't quite understand. Is it pity? Is it sympathy? "Nevermind. It's stupid," he mumbles.

I don't push. Perhaps because I don't want to hear what he has to say. The outside world isn't like this place. Outside they have families and friends and lives that mean something.

To think there is anything bad outside those walls eats away at my desire to leave. And leaving is supposed to be my new purpose in life. We have to get out of here soon. Without Tobias, there's a good chance we will both be on that bus to Auction next Reaping. I won't let it happen to us.

We get into our hideout, tossing our stuff into a box in the corner. Charles collapses on his blanket, burying his face into a pillow. Though it's covered in sand, it's home.

I sit down on a broken chair we've fixed with ripped books, tossing my sandals with other pairs of shoes we've found in the wasteland. There are candles on a wooden table, and I light one up so it isn't pitch black back here. It's a new moon, and it's cloudy. It might be the poorest home in this world, but it's loved.

Charles surprisingly falls asleep. I'm relieved I don't have to pretend anymore, and all the false happiness leaves my face. I sit comatose, staring at the wall.

I've fucked us. How are we going to survive?

Light seemed to think I could join his clan, but that was before Hail was killed. I don't think they would be as welcoming. He also wants me to talk to a friend of his. They might be able to protect me when I do another stupid thing.

Too much of Tobias breathes into my thoughts. I can survive without him.

Tobias is not the end all to my existence, but what am I without him? I'm just a Rat.

No, I'm an ember to the flames.

—

28

Downfall

Looking back at all of it, I realize it had all been my fault. From the beginning to the end, had I done everything just slightly different, I wouldn't be here and I wouldn't be about to die. If I had done little trivial things, everything could have been prevented.

Monday morning came without incident. We had survived the weekend despite how Tobias was so sure we wouldn't. I defied him and made it through. It was the proof I needed to gain the confidence to survive on my own.

Sixty hours of sweating added up, so our priority was a shower. I bought us new clothes. I wore shorts and a tank top and stood in front of the mirror with a big smile. It was the most revealing outfit I've ever owned, but I felt invincible.

On the sink, there was a black scrunchy. It belonged to someone. I was going to walk away from it. But what would it feel like to have my long, heavy hair free from my face? Tobias never wanted me to change my hair; now was my biggest opportunity to show him up. Not only did I make it through the weekend without him, but I'm becoming my own person.

So I took it.

I walked into class with a bit of pep in my step. I held my head high for the first time, smiling, meeting people's gaze with imprudence. Nothing could bring me down today. Not even their whispers.

When class was over, I didn't wait and hide. I joined the rest of the students in the hallway, clambering down the stairs in a sea of bodies. I noticed Light standing with a group of his clan at the bottom of the staircase. He looked at me, his words fading on his lips. I didn't have to turn away. I boldly met his gaze, allowing the excitement he stirred in me to show.

Charles jumped and waved above the taller group, and I walked by Light, trying not to stumble when he smiled back. I grabbed Charles' hand and we headed out of the building.

"Hey." A girl called, and at first, I didn't know she was talking to me, so I ignored it until she grabbed my arm, twisting me around. A teenager from Coal stared back at me. She was not beautiful in the least. She had cold black eyes, braided blond hair, and a clan tattoo on her cheek. She was tall and lanky with big manly hands. "You got something, Rat?" she held her hand out expectantly.

"No," I turned back around.

She grabbed me again, and I yanked defensively. "Give it to me or I'll mess you up more than your pimp."

"Fuck off." I tugged Charles along, trying to escape the situation, but the girl wouldn't let it go.

She snatched my hair, pulling me back into her chest. "Give me my fucking tie."

Instincts kicked in. I elbowed her in the stomach, and she released her grip. I faced her with Charles behind me. The students were quickly encircling us like a dinner pit. My escape was gone.

"Ember, let's go," Charles pulled on my arm, but he didn't know we no longer had Tobias' protection. I had to show the school that I was capable of protecting myself. This would be an excellent way to warn them not to mess with me. A fight, one-on-one, where death wasn't allowed- I could win.

"Let's go, then," the girl insisted.

"Get her, Cinder!" Dark shades of black and gray consumed the space behind her as Coal members gathered. Cinder had the support of dozens while the most notable members were standing off in the distance; Ash and his bodyguard sat on top of the stairs for a good view.

I had no one but Charles. But I didn't need anyone else.

I attacked, running bent over. I slammed into her stomach, knocking her to the ground. She pounded her fists on my back and used her legs to get me off. I rolled in the dirt, trying to get up before she attacked, but she jumped on me. Her nails dug into my head, ripping my scalp and pulling my hair. I cried out as I swung my whole arm and slammed my wide fist into her knee. Cinder grunted, faltering. I shoved her off, watching her limp as she tried to keep to her feet. I attacked while she's distracted. My arms wailing, hoping to catch her face but Cinder covered her head, throwing herself away and rolled on the floor.

I didn't try to catch my breath. I kept going like a bulldozer. I pulled my leg back to kick her, but she grabbed my foot and pulled my leg out from under me. My head hit the floor, and my hands gripped my head as a tidal wave of blackness drowned me.

I couldn't recover fast enough. Cinder crawled on top of me and grabbed my head again and started banging it into the ground. My consciousness was weakened in pain. The more she dropped my head into the dirt, the less I comprehended. The ache blackened my sight, my strength was waning by the moment, and I thought I was going to die.

With a swipe of the air, the girl was gone.

Just like that.

My hopeful belief was she had given up or gotten what she wanted and left me alone with my pain. Then I remembered Charles.

"Charles!" I screamed, sitting up half in a daze. I searched for him, but I needn't look far.

He was standing above her, and a butterfly knife was in his hands.

Where did that knife come from?

There was blood. It was dripping from the blade and Charles' hands. The girl lay motionless on the ground, with blood all over her. There was so much red paint I couldn't determine where it was coming from. And as I struggled to get closer, it became clear to me. Charles stabbed her.

I crawled forward, hoping for a way to save her.

But when I touched Cinder's fingers, someone grabbed me. The noise was deafening, screams and curses filling my ears while I was pulled away from the dying girl. No one was helping her, and I couldn't figure out why

She was dying! Why weren't they saving her?

My feet dragged in the sand as I fought against them, trying to get back to the girl on the floor but they shoved and forced me forward till my knees hit the dirt. I caught myself from falling, staring at the ground.

It hit me.

Charles murdered a girl.

Charles murdered a girl on school property.

Charles murdered a girl on school property in front of Coal members.

There was no escaping it. The rules were simple. Yet the rules I hadn't taught him. Things like killing I never spoke about. I never wanted him to know of those evils. I wanted him to stay innocent.

So one of us was.

Now it's over.

I sit back on my heels. Charles is beside me, struggling against the kids holding his arms. I attempt to catch his eyes. I want him to know I tried to protect him. I tried to do what was best for him. I wanted to apologize for everything I didn't do. For everything I didn't say.

The schoolyard quiets down. It had been so unbelievably loud, and now I could hear the ringing in my ears. Charles is huffing and puffing. He's my little brother, and even at this moment, I'm amazed by him. He's more formidable than I gave him credit for. He never needed me at all. I needed him.

Charles glances up and stills. I don't need to look to know who it is.

Tobias.

On top of the stairs, with Ash beside him, he peers down at me dressed in black like the grim reaper. I thought he'd be smug with his constant smirk, but the expression on his face is like the day he killed Hail. It's full of emotion that doesn't match the monster.

His eyes slip towards Charles, and his face transforms into the evil I know so well.

Tobias reaches into his vest and takes out his gun.

29

Loss

"Tobias, don't!"

My body slams into the ground. A knee digs into my back. I push against it, but they put all their weight on me, and I can't get up. I can only watch as Tobias' black steel toed boots slowly descend the stairs.

My heart is pounding. My world is crashing. "Please. I'll do anything. I'll be with you. Please"

I cry, and I beg. Everything he always wanted from me, I give freely now.

Take it, take it all. I don't care.

I turn my head with my cheek against the dirt. Charles is looking at me. His big bright green eyes can shine so beautifully when he's happy. But there is no happiness in his gaze now. No light.

There is a gun against his temple. I thought he would fight it. Throw a random fist or curse out anyone near.

My wild boy. My best friend. My brother.

Tears blind my vision. But I can make out the soft smile on

his thin lips.

My words tremble as I speak, "Please, don't."

And then the gun fires. I flinch, my eyes widening. Charles' knees give out, and he drops heavily to the ground. His face hits the dirt. His gaze is even with mine, but he doesn't see me.

I watch consciousness dwindle out of his eyes, those glistening young, naive eyes until his gaze is dull and sightless. His lips, which were usually spread wide with excitement, are left open as blood trickles out. His breath exhales a final time, and there is no more life.

Incoherent sobs are all that's left of me. I can't feel or think. The pain in my back disappears, and I'm on my hands and knees, crawling toward him. I don't pretend I can save him. I don't lie to myself and say he is still with me. I know that Charles is gone.

My shaking fingers reach out and touch his dark skin. He's still warm, like coals after the fire has been extinguished. I roll him over. His body is heavy and limp. I rest his head on my lap. Blood continues to flow from the hole in his temple, dripping down my bare legs. I stroke his soft stubs of hair while I hum a song I don't know.

Every mistake repeats in my head. It's an avalanche of blame and self-hate mingling with chaotic denial.

Come back.
I'm so stupid
Don't go.
Why did I fight?
Wake up.
I'm sorry.
The sky darkens.
Hours go by.

My knees ache. My body aches, and my heart aches. But I can't let go. He was everything. Without him, there is nowhere to go. Nothing to do.

Stranger hands are pulling at his arms. A person that collects dead bodies. I grip Charles' clothes, but the man pulls at my hands, pushing me away. I'm exhausted, and any fight I had doesn't surface as I watch motionless. Charles' body is placed on a gurney, and two men lift it by the handles and walk away.

I look around. The school is empty, and I'm alone sitting in the dirt in front of the school steps. 'Myers School for the Unwanted' reads above the double doors. I stare at the last word.

Unwanted.

Unwanted.

Charles was wanted.

I touch the blood on my legs. Charles' life fluid decorating me like a blanket.

I stare off after the man that took my little brother, wondering if I left now, I could still catch up to him and keep Charles' body with me. I could rest him at home and let him sleep in our house. And somehow, through that, he would actually be with me again.

Yet I can't move. I am too afraid if I left this spot, I would lose what is left of Charles. I lay down, hugging the ground, imagining I could hear Charles' heartbeat.

Footsteps scrape against the floor and stop beside me. "I had to."

It is Tobias' voice. Tears and anger flood my chest, but I say nothing.

He kneels beside me and whispers, "I'm not a bad man, Scream. Everything I do, everything I've done, has been for you. I told you Ash would want revenge. I did what I could. But now I have nothing left to give. I can't protect you anymore."

Bile rises in my throat. How can someone stand before me and say that after everything he's done? What kind of human being is he?

My silence touches on his temper. "Guess I won't get a thank you."

My eyes finally lift to him. I am beyond words. Nothing would form. A thought of Kevin runs through my head. Is this why he chose to be mute? He knows how meaningless words really are but if Tobias looked closely enough he'd see the promise in my eyes. The promise that I'll end his life the same way he ended Charles'.

Tobias meets my gaze for only a second or two before flipping his sight away. "Yea, I didn't think so," he mumbles to himself. "You're nothing, really. Don't get why I cared so much."

He steps around Charles' blood-soaked bed. I glance around for the knife Charles used, but it is gone. Everything is gone.

"And if you think you can hide in that *secret hideout*, you're dumber than I thought."

I think about throwing myself at him, wailing my fists anywhere I could, and hoping something kills him. Or if I attack him, would he shoot me too?

* * *

When I leave Charles' saturated pile of blood, I have nowhere to go. Miss Nancy locks the gates, eyeing me through the fence. She doesn't know what happened or doesn't care. As she waddles away, I cling to the fence and find Charles' bloodstain in the distance.

He is my home. Whatever is left of him is my home.

Where would they take him?

The Wastelands.

I run with desperation. The Wastelands close at six, and the sun is low in the sky. I need to make it, to find him, and bring him back home. He deserves to lay on his bed, wrapped in his blankets.

Would I be able to find him?

I trip and fall. My chin hits the dirt, my teeth biting hard on my bottom lip, cutting it painfully. I ignore it, crawling in the dirt. I don't have time to wallow. I have to make it.

Someone kicks me in the stomach. I roll on my side, curling into myself.

Leaning over me with a smile is Cloud. "Where do you think you're going?" He grabs my wrists and pulls, dragging my body through the sand, but he's bringing me the wrong way. Charles is waiting for me in the Wastelands; I don't have much time. I twist away, reaching.

Cloud kicks me again against my legs. A punch to the face. The ground shifts, and dizziness swirls.

Even as my heart thumps, trying to wake my body to react, I can't. The sun has set. The Wastelands are closed, and Charles is gone.

It's over.

Cloud stands above me, undoing his belt. "I'm gonna end this rebellion by getting rid of you. But first, I'm gonna—" Cloud looks above me, "Who the fuck are you?"

I stretch my hand out. Out of the alley, I can make out a shadow. It's got to be Charles. He's waiting for me. He always waits for me even when I don't want him to. I crawl towards them.

My awesome little brother.

Cloud stumbles backward, holding his loose pants. "The Rebellion has a Special? Are you fucking kidding me?"

My fingers claw in the sand as I pull myself forward. There is a pair of white, dirt-free shoes beside me, and I pass by whoever it is with my eyes out straight where Charles is reaching out a hand to take me home.

30

Broken

My footsteps are numbing and short, carrying a burden of dead weight upon them. I've been wandering like a ghost that can't get into heaven. I'm in purgatory, unsure if I want to live but too afraid to die.

It's the middle of the night, a time I would never journey. I keep my arms wrapped around me, surprised by the cold. My broken lips tremble as I put one foot in front of the other.

One thing is clear. There was a difference between Charles and me. I thought I didn't belong here. I began to believe I was a mistake, that they had grabbed the wrong girl. But that's not true, is it? I'm unwanted, filled with vileness in me. I'm exactly where I'm supposed to be.

Charles was the mistake. And God, or whoever decides, rectified that mistake and took him away.

I stand in front of the Rain building. The lights shine on the ground, nearly blinding in this darkness. The guards at the gate nervously twitter, waiting for me. "Light," I whisper, my voice raw and tired.

They look at each other, but eventually, one nods, and the other says, "Follow me."

Inside I stare at nothing but the blue carpet as my dirty feet sink into it. We travel up the stairs. It's a mammoth of a building, but what is time to me now? I have nowhere to be.

We stop, and it isn't long till the man in front mumbles something and knocks for me.

That's when Light opens the door.

I won't lift my eyes to see his face. I'm too ashamed.

"You asked me to do you a favor if she showed. You got your end of the deal?"

Movement occurs, and a plastic bag passes between their hands. "Can you send up a doctor?"

Light touches my arm, and I step into the room. It's a small apartment with a kitchen and living room. It smells like him.

I bow my head, regretting coming here.

"Hey, Light. If Drop hears about this…"

"Yeah, I know."

The door shuts.

I keep my head down. I don't know what he knows or what he saw. I'm to blame for all of it, and if he felt the same, I couldn't handle it, not now. "Ember."

I shake my head.

Don't call me that. I'm no one's ember.

He presses a hand against my back and leads me down the hallway. My feet move on their own. I'm an empty tortoise shell, and he guides me, turning into the bathroom. "You should wash up."

Should I?

I can't find the energy to do it. I want to curl into a ball and sleep forever.

"I could... help. Or get someone." When he turns to go, I reach for his fingers. There isn't anyone else that I trust. I'm putting myself in his hands, hoping he'll know how to fix me because I don't.

His big hands take the sleeves of my shirt and tug light, asking for permission. I would have laughed at this. Like I had anything to hide or any care left at all.

I wince as he pulls the shirt over my head, a soft groan breaking through. I had forgotten I was in a fight. There are bruises on my ribs and my back. Open sores on my knees and elbows. My knuckles are swollen and my head hasn't stopped pounding.

Cinder.

Another death on my hands.

"God," Light frets, drinking in all my injuries. "Jesus Christ, how are you standing?"

I don't know.

It's never been 'how'. It's been 'have to'.

I have to keep standing.

I hold onto his shoulder as he removes my blood-soaked shorts. They are stiff like old bread. I stare at them, the last bit of Charles I'll ever possess again.

Light disappears from my peripheral. I stand shivering in my bra and panties. The water turns on with its squeaky pipes. When he returns, he grabs my useless arm and brings me over to the tub. I sway with a wave of dizziness, and Light catches me before I fall. I rest my head against his shoulder. The contact is like the grace of a feather. It is soft and welcoming, but it's undeserved.

I force my feet beneath me.

"When was the last time you ate anything?"

I can't remember what day it is.

With his assistance, I step into the bath. The warmth shocks my senses, the water sizzling my wounds. I pass out, hoping never to wake up again.

* * *

My heart seizes, and I wake, panting in my fear. My eyes are wild and crazy, searching my surroundings. Where am I? Am I safe? Is Charles Okay?

They are the main questions I asked myself for weeks. Thinking of Charles reopens the gates of pain, and I curl, crying, sobbing. I don't want to get out of bed. I want to waste away and never rise again.

It feels like I can go on forever, but I'm not able to. I don't know where I am, and though my grief buries much care, survival has always been ingrained in me. It's what makes me move.

When I throw off the covers, my fear explodes. I'm wearing a light blue cotton gown. Bandages cover my arms and parts of my legs and I begin to pick at it, annoyed by the itch. My hair feels cold and clumpy, barely dry and tangled.

None of my surroundings look familiar. I am in a room I had only seen in the Rain's bathhouse. I lay on a giant bed with a big thick white quilt with blue pillows. There is a nightstand with a cup of water. A desk is off to one side, and pictures hang on the wall of people in blue and white shirts.

Definitely Rain.

The bathroom light is on, guiding me to it. Dirt and blood decorate the tiled floor. The big white tub is stained with blood, giving it a rust tint.

Memories start to return.

Light helped me into the tub. He saw me partially naked.

My cheeks heat up, and I pull my shirt to look down. My bra is gone. Did he undress me further? A hand covers my mouth, suppressing embarrassment and disgust.

I sit on the bed but move to the chair instead. I can't believe I came here.

I wasn't thinking. I should go.

I touch the gauze on my knuckles. The memory of the fight replays with horrible accuracy. I can make out the blood, the screams, the cries.

My cries.

I didn't realize I was in such bad shape. Feeling nothing had its perks, the emptiness in my gut hadn't been noticeable but now in the aftermath, the agony of it all is too heavy.

Light got a medic for me. Does he think I could pay him back? Or does he expect to be repaid in other ways, like Tobias would want?

When I see the door knob jiggle, I keep myself from running. I am in his debt and know better than to run from it. The hunting and chasing that would follow me wouldn't be worth it.

Light opens the door, peeking in. When he finds me sitting on the stool, he lets the door fall open, leaning against the doorway. He has his hands in the pockets of gray sweatpants and a white tank, dressed like he just woke up.

Where was he when Charles was killed? Was he watching like he watched Cloud hit me? Was he watching like he had been when Hail was murdered? The resentment I feel for everyone that was there becomes overwhelming, and I bite,

"What do you want?"

"What do you mean?" he sighs as if he is disappointed. I hate that tone.

"For helping me, what do you want?"

"Jeezes, girl. I don't want anything from you."

"Did you take it already?"

His black brows knit, "Are you accusing me of..of touching you after I helped you?"

I bow my head, clenching my teeth.

He calms himself down, gently speaking, "The medic was a girl, and she dressed you."

Now I feel like an idiot.

I know I should apologize, but his world and mine are two completely different things. It's not illogical in my world. Being a clan member, he could never understand.

"You should eat."

"I should go."

"You need to rest."

"Don't tell me what I need."

I can feel his eyes, but I don't move my gaze from the floor. I'm angry, and though I know it has nothing to do with him, I can't stop being angry.

Light goes to the dresser and digs into the drawer. He slams it shut, making me flinch. He throws clothes on the bed.

"Go back to sleep," he snags the doorknob and is about to shut it when he stalls. He looks at me, but only a second when he drops his head, "I'm sorry about Charles."

When the door closes, my knees give out, and my tears bust through so suddenly that I start coughing. I stay crumbled on the floor, crying into the carpet, a softer comfort than sand.

31

Friends

I snuggled in the blankets after I woke up. Light must have picked me up from the floor and put me here because I don't remember. His scent soaks into the pillows, and it swiftly becomes addicting. It's comforting during a time when I am more alone than I've ever been. The ball of disgust dwelling in my chest is weakened momentarily and I'm able to think of something else other than Charles.

Revenge.

How do I get it? And who do I focus on first?

Tobias?

Or Ash?

I sit up. I'm hungry and in pain. I have to go to the bathroom, and I'm beyond thirsty. All of it combined reminds me of my first week here. It's a time I try so hard to forget, but it sticks around like dirt under the nails.

I'm dressed in oversized flannel pants that tie tight to my waist to keep from falling. A long sleeve shirt wraps around me, and I have to pull the sleeves up to bring out my hands. My bandages itch, and I pick at them.

I shut the door to the bathroom. I stare at the lock, forever enchanted by such a thing.

I find a disposable toothbrush waiting, and I use it. I can't help but sneak glances at all of Light's trinkets. There's cologne, deodorant, lotion, and a collection of watches.

I squirt some lotion on my hands, smell it, and spread it along my skin.

What would life be like, living here?

Though my body begs for it, I don't go back to bed. My hand instead rests on the doorknob, hesitant. I think about what I'm going to say because our last conversation didn't go so well.

Light deserves gratitude. Despite how rude I was, he still treated me better than Tobias.

I exit the bedroom and travel lightly down the hall. The carpet disguises my footsteps, and it feels pleasant against my toes. I can hear people talking, but it sounds funny. It's not real, like the voices over the intercom.

I lean against the wall when I get to the intersection. The TV is on, another contraption he so easily possesses.

Light sits on the couch and laughs. It's a pleasant sound, a deep sound from the gut. It isn't like Charles' laughter, which is high-pitched and nasally. I rest my head back against the wall, suppressing tears as I think about the laugh I'll never hear again.

Step by step, I shuffle till Light sees me.

His eyes widen, and he hurriedly turns the TV off. He gets to his feet, nervously rubbing his hands on his pants before he catches himself. He straightens and clears his throat. "You hungry?"

Light dashes over to the kitchen without waiting for an answer, his head sticking in the refrigerator. "The doctor said something light. So I've got oatmeal." He goes about making it. I've never had oatmeal, but whatever he is willing to give me, I couldn't deny it.

He sets up a place at the kitchen table and pulls the chair out. When I stay still, not knowing what he is doing, he moves back into the kitchen and brings the bowl to the placemat. "Some water too," he speaks to himself, grabbing a bottle from the fridge. He puts that down as well.

I haven't yet moved.

"Well, come on, sit," Light gestures to the chair.

He acts like it is natural. Like sitting and eating a meal so nicely given is something I do every day.

But that's what's wrong with me, not him.

I bring myself over and sit.

"You should take this." I keep an eye on his movements, and he empties a pill onto his hand, resting it next to my water. "It will help with the pain."

Whenever I was given a pain pill, it was a sign that the worst was over. I wish it were true.

I drink the entire bottle of water, swallowing the Tylenol. Light rushes to get me another one. I stare at the oatmeal, and my belly rumbles. I want to eat, but the hole in my chest doesn't care enough . When the hot glob of substance touches my tongue, I hiss. I hear him chuckle lightly, saying, "Blow on it to cool it down."

I stare at it.

I don't want the food. I don't want to be here. I don't want to be anywhere that Charles can't be.

I snap up, and I search wildly for an exit. I have no idea where I am or how to get out. Since I woke, the instincts I honed over the last four months have been absent. I'm vulnerable because of the destruction Charles' death caused.

Wake up, damn it. I'm alone in a room with a member of a clan that hates me. My instincts finally come alive. I run back into the bedroom, slamming the door. I swing around, trying to find something to block it with. There is no time. Light is already at the door, calling me, asking what's wrong.

I head to the bathroom, shutting that door too. I hurry for the window, pulling at it, trying to yank it open. It won't budge, and by the time my hand finds the lock, Light is there grabbing me by the shoulders, forcefully turning me around. I yell curses, and I beg, I fight, and I struggle.

I'm alive again. This is how it should be. Fighting for my life.

Light's voice barrels through my panic, "Stop. Please stop."

I don't stop. I can't. I smack and twist and shove.

"I'll go, I'll go," he backs away from me as I lower myself into the cold bathtub, seeking any refuge I can. Horror and confusion spread over his face. He presses a hand against his mouth.

"I'll go. I'm sorry," Light turns and walks away.

Panting, alone, cold, and dazed, I sit there. My body shakes in the sudden adrenaline, and my heart pounds in the aftermath.

I let my legs stretch out, resting in the tub, shivering against its cold skin.

I don't belong here in this lovely, cozy room with its privacy and warmth. I find myself yearning for the outside. Because it is out there that I understand. It is outside in the violent world I am made for.

Light wouldn't understand. I don't want him to. In the same way, I never wanted Charles to understand the bad things. Light and I are not meant to cross paths. He's clean and whole.

I'm dirty and broken.

Kevin will understand me and I think about heading toward him, but he is unreachable. I will never see Tobias again until I can kill him. However long that will take.

I get up. I go out into the living room and find Light leaning against the kitchen counter, staring at the untouched bowl of food, trying to figure out where he had gone wrong.

"Hey."

His eyes snap up wide in surprise. He straightens, coming to me. "I'm-" The moment I back up, he stops mid-stride. "Whatever I did, I'm sorry, I—'

I force a smile, "It's not you."

"I thought oatmeal would be okay—"

I laugh weakly, "It's not that either." He is utterly confused. I shake my head, "I shouldn't be here. I don't belong here."

"Your injuries-"

"It doesn't matter," I whisper. "Everything you've done has been wonderful. I'll repay you if—"

"No, I don't want—"

"Thank you," I finally managed to get out. If he doesn't want anything in return, at least he can have my gratitude. I don't give it lightly. "I should go." Finding the exit this time is easy without panic blurring my vision.

I look back at Light. His gaze is on me, mournful. He wants me to stay but knows better than to try. Charles and Light are from the same stack. The world I live in isn't meant for people like them.

Staying any longer, I'd lose my nerve. For a short time I've been here, I saw a life that would never be in my grasp. I need to leave before I let it seep into my veins.

"Ember," he calls. I love the sound of my name on his lips.

Light smiles, and it lights up his blue eyes. "We're friends, okay?"

Friends. No. We're not friends. Friends have similar hopes and dreams. Friends have a connection bringing them together. Friends chase you around in the Wastelands and wish to be nowhere else.

But I smile at him and nod my head. I hope he won't be too hurt when I never look at him again.

32

Revival

It's early morning. In an hour, the Coal guards will leave their post, and I'll be able to get into my hideout.

I dread it.

The home Charles and I made will still have the impression of his footsteps in the sand. His blanket and pillow will be as they were when he woke. His dirty pile of clothes will be in the hamper, and the little toys he's found in the Wastelands will remain on a crappy broken table.

And within the walls, his laughter will echo. All our conversations in the dark will resonate like the droning of an air conditioner.

I find myself at the playground. My hand reaches for the rusty metal chain of the swing, a place I used to sit and watch Charles as he swung on the monkey bars. If I hadn't done so many things wrong, he would be here right now. The guilt is thicker than I can handle. Tears fall, and a sob breaks out. Before I know it, I'm curled up in a ball at the base of the swing screaming into my hands.

I stay there, even as my tears fade, leaving me empty. I stare at the stars trying to find Charles' ghost.

Isn't God a ghost? Will they be together?

When the sky lightens, I know I missed my chance to go to the hideout. I'm not ready to go there without Charles.

My stomach forces me to my feet. My head is foggy and dizzy from so much stupid crying that I stumble as I walk. I drag along my heavy body that is being pulled to the earth.

I get a food tray and slap it down on a table far from where Charles and I always sat. Food isn't easy to swallow when the body doesn't want to do any work, so only a few bits of chicken make it to my stomach. I give up before too long and push it away, resting my head on the table where I finally sleep.

* * *

Too soon, noise wakes me. Kids are piling into the cafeteria, telling me school let out. I must have been sleeping for hours. I leave, not bothering to throw out my food.

"Scream," Zack calls, but I ignore it, continuing my sluggish pace without a glance back. I'm too tired to pretend he isn't disgusting and frightening at the same time.

I pass the Rain Compound, pass the Teacher's Lounge, pass the school, pass Boundary and Rat buildings. My feet led me back to our alleyway. There are guards posted because it's still early. I sit against the Rat building, with my head on my knees, and wait.

When they leave their post, I still don't move. Part of me wants to stay away forever. The other part wants to see if Charles is there waiting for me.

Walking down the dark hallway, I expect him to come

around the corner with his brilliant smile and light green eyes shining, playing it off like it had been a big joke. But I'm not stupid enough to really believe it. Don't know why my heart is beating so fast. And when I turn the corner, and nothing greets me, I sink to my knees in the dirt.

It's destroyed. Someone had come through here and taken everything. I can't even plunge into Charles' blanket because it's gone. All the trinkets we found in the Wastelands, the clothes, the shoes, the little toys; it's all gone.

Even the hole we've spent hours digging is filled again.

They erased him.

My hands ball into fists on my thighs.

I want revenge. I want revenge so badly I can taste it on my tongue.

What I want more is to be with Charles. I want to apologize for keeping everything from him. For never confiding in him. For believing that if I kept the world from him, it would never hurt him.

I'm such a fucking idiot.

I want to die.

Why did I stick around this world so long? Nothing will get better, no matter how much I want it to be. It's not worth all the suffering I have to do every day to survive. Even revenge isn't enough to keep going.

Vengeance is impossible. Tobias is too strong. He'll win, like he's won every time. He's a bigger monster than I can ever be.

My fingers spread in the sand. I will end it. One little thing to cut the strings. That is all I need. Nothing much. A sharp rock, a pointed twig, a stray piece of glass. Something so small and overlooked. Like Charles was.

Anything. Anything there is to end my life.

My fingers twist and sink deeper. My heart beats faster, desperate now for something to end this. There has to be something.

God, anything. I have never called out to you before, never in my whole fucking existence. I am asking now. Give me something to end my life. Please, please let me be with Charles.

God!

"What are you–"

I swing around, landing hard on my back.

"Looking for?"

I kick at the dirt, pushing myself far away until I hit the wall hard.

The stranger puts up his hands, "I'm not gonna hurt ya." He laughs, "Probably heard that one before." The boy squats down, burying the flashlight in the dirt so the bright beam shoots up to the sky. He wears a ripped black long-sleeve shirt and cut-off black shorts. His hands, shaking, are wrapped in gloves with the tips cut off showing his blackened nails. His hair is short, and he shakes his head to get the bangs from his face. With the light I can make out one clear distinction about him: his eyes are green. Just as Charles' eyes had been. "I've been waiting for you. Name's Shakes," he puts out a hand, but I don't even glance at it. My attention is well-trained. I can make out the rope he dropped in on. The decaying combat boots on his feet. He may be a Rat, but he is a wealthy Rat. Or a highly dangerous one.

He has my only exit.

But why fight? If I'm ready to die, maybe this kid, this reincarnation of Charles, has been sent to help me.

"Sorry about Charles," Shakes throws out, "He was a good kid."

"How do you know him?"

"I didn't. But I heard enough. He's been trying to get me to talk to you."

"And who the hell are you?"

"Someone that could help."

I scoff at the absurdity, "I don't need help."

He chuckles, "It's funny. There's a rumor you're stubborn. Let me explain."

I notice his hands trembling. I observe his face, searching for the fear he is displaying, but there isn't any. No nervousness or anxiety. But hands don't shake for no reason. I catch a lump in his shirt, oddly shaped. Either a gun or a big knife. Though dirty, his face has no scratches, bruises, or scars. He is well protected.

"Scream."

My attention snaps back to him.

"Do you got a different name? I don't like calling you that."

To ask such a question, eases a bit of the tension. I swallow the misery in my throat, wondering when it will ever go away.

"Ember."

"Ember. That's…pretty good. I hate my name too, but," he holds up his trembling hands, "It suits me fine, I guess. I saw you looking. I have tremors. I can't seem to help it." Shakes leans back and falls on his butt. A position an attacker would never take.

My tense muscles relax slightly. "What do you want?"

"That's a loaded question. I guess I'll start simple. Do you know who you are?"

The simple question pisses me off. I'm alive, and Charles is dead because someone out there thinks I'm someone. "No, and it doesn't matter. Leave me alone."

He studies me longer than I like, and I fidget under his stare. "How can I believe you?"

I cackle maliciously, "I don't give a fuck what you believe. Get out of here!"

His green eyes flick up to the camera, and out of curiosity, I glance at it too. The red dot is gone, and only darkness remains.

Where did it go?

I watch Shakes. Did he manage to shut off the camera? If there was interest left in this world, I'd be curious, but I can't force myself to care. I need to be left alone to do what I should have done months ago.

"No one can hear you but me."

The implication is a siren in my head.

Shakes winces, "That didn't sound right." He scratches his temple. "I meant the teachers aren't watching right now. So if you want to tell me something you can."

Another person wants memories I don't have.

"Barking up the wrong tree."

He studies me, waiting for something I don't have to give him. He restarts his attempt, "The clan I'm in—"

"I don't want to be in any clan."

"It's a different kind of clan. Not many people know it exists."

"It doesn't matter," I cut off any more conversation, standing up. "I don't want it."

Shakes gets up too. He's only a few inches taller than me, not much bigger in size. I could fight him and perhaps win, but I'm too tired to try, and I don't want to win.

"If it is the end, Ember."

I'm frozen by him.

How could he know I'm at the edge?

"Then it wouldn't matter if you just came with me for a couple minutes."

I glance around at my destroyed home. I've nothing left to do in this life, it's pointless to even try to begin again. But Charles and Light both tried to get me to see something that I refused. Maybe this boy is who or what they wanted me to find. I owe it to both of them.

I nod, and he turns, leading the way out, leaving the flashlight in the dirt. I look over the bare remains of my happiest moments but there is nothing left for me here. I step after him, taking a wild risk.

At the edge of the building, I'm about to warn him of the Coal members but he steps out and turns to wait for me. No one is there.

Did he have something to do with that?

From the moon's height, it is now the middle of the night, a dangerous time for predators. The only lights come from Coal behind us and Boundary further down the street. There are long shadows dancing on the ground, mostly hidden behind buildings. They move like hunting hyenas, jumping from one hole to the next, following our progress.

Why don't they attack?

I stand behind Shakes and slightly to the side, exposing a partial view of his face. He walks with an air of fearlessness only clan leaders possess. There is a smile on his lips as if he doesn't know how to frown. He strolls along, ignorant, and I find him so odd.

The facts aren't adding up. There is no one indestructible. Shakes either isn't real, which in all cases could very well be true. Or he hasn't been here long enough, and the blind is leading the blind.

"How long have you been here?"

He scrunches his face in concentration, humming his thoughts. "About five years."

My instincts flash in a warning. If Shakes is lying to me, chances are he means me harm. I need to run. The onlookers in the dark stop me from taking immediate action. If they are part of his clan, I won't get very far. I need to be calculating with my escape plan.

I allow more space between us. A few extra feet. If he chooses to turn on me, I at least will see it coming.

Shakes tilts his head back to face the sky. "Zack took good care of us in the beginning."

I have trouble seeing lies from the truth. I'm too ignorant of life around me to spot the difference. And Shakes is very believable. To mention Zack, a figure no one wants to know, reveals a secret to me. He trusted Zack like I had and got burned.

How could anyone last five years here?

Tobias did.

"I was with the first shipment. This place was different then. Just ten of us. It was fun for a while."

"Were you friends with Tobias?"

His smile fades, and he doesn't answer right away. Our footsteps are the only sound in the night. Even something simple as walking exposes the difference between us. His footsteps are sure and steady, while mine shuffle with uncertainty. "Yeah. I was. We all were a family for a time. I used to call him brother."

The thought disgusts me. Who could ever see Tobias as someone to love?

"How did you stay alive?"

He shakes his head, looking back at me with a smile on his

lips. "I didn't. I died a few times." Shakes chuckles to himself, "Figure of speech."

A big spotlight brightens the area at Boundary's entrance. Two guards stand on the stairs, watching us. Shakes walks toward the steps, greeting the guards with familiarity. I'm not as bold as him. Boundary has never been friendly but I step into the light, holding a hand to block the brightness. When I lower it, Shakes faces me with a gun at his side.

I'm frozen like a bunny as a wolf creeps toward it. I thought for a moment, Charles was leading me. He knew how to bring the best out of me even though he didn't know it. He gave me purpose, and all I want is to find it again.

Shakes raises the gun, the barrel pointing straight at me. Despite his shaking before, his stance is polished and motionless. His features are in darkness behind the mask clan members wear so well.

I'm not surprised by his move. Clan members have no loyalty to anyone but their clan.

What does shock me is the way my heart beats. Erratically, frantically, pumping so fiercely I can hear it in my ears. It is fear that causes such a reaction.

I'm scared to die.

Do I still have hope this world will get better?

I thought I was ready. I have nothing left in this place. So why do I want to live?

I want to know my name.

He fires, the bullet striking the ground next to me and spraying dirt. The noise echoes in the vastness of the night.

My knees hit the floor.

"Good," he whispers. "You're not done yet."

My hands catch me as I lean forward, panting, my mouth

watering with the rise of nausea.

I glare at him.

Shakes approaches, and I lean back on my heels. He kneels down in front of me and grips my jaw. I sneer, attempting to pull away, but he keeps me steady by pressing the barrel against my temple. It's hot from its recent use. "I have to know something, and I need you to tell me the truth." His voice is dark, far different from how he greeted me. "What do you feel for Tobias?"

"Tobias?" I question, swallowing the bile. "What is he?"

"If I told you he could get you out of here, what would you say?"

I flick my eyes over Shakes' face. I want him to see it, everything I feel for that monster of a kid. Charles' death destroyed any chance of me ever going to Tobias for anything. Even if it meant my freedom.

"I will find my own way."

Shakes grins, and stands up, holding his trembling hand out for me. "That's good to hear."

Whatever trust this brat had been trying to build no longer applies. Pointing a gun at me had been his mistake. I ignore his hand, staying on my knees. "What do you want with me?"

Shakes' hand falls. He puts his gun back under his shirt, explaining, "Honesty is a hard thing to find here. The only way my clan has been kept secret is because I have tested every single member in trust. I could not bring you any further until I knew who you were. And now I know."

"Oh yea?" I scoff, "And who am I?"

"Exactly who I need. You will get us out of here."

I shake my head; he is obviously looking in the wrong place. "I don't remember anything. I'm not the person you want. I'm no one.

He squats, grabbing at one of my hands and holding it tight within his own. He is warm.

Charles had always been warm.

It is odd being so close to this stranger without fear. And I realize quickly that I do not fear him. His eyes are easy to read, and his hands are small, almost the same size as my own. I imagine Charles' hands would have been like this when he had gotten older.

"People like us, Ember, are who the teachers want to destroy. We lack greed. The hate. The lust. We don't belong here. We are a mistake and they know it." My eyes shut, and tears well up. To hear someone else say it, to believe it strikes my heart at its weakness. I bob my head, tears spilling down my cheeks. "I can't promise we'll ever get out. But I can promise revenge. I can promise redemption. You and I can damage the world they've forced upon us, and together, we can stop little kids like Charles from suffering at their hands."

I rub snot on the back of my hand. His words are filling the emptiness inside my heart. He's building it with stone instead of sand. I can feel it strengthen me. "How?"

"Look me in the eye."

I force my gaze on his. The confidence inside him is pouring out and I'm drinking it in.

"You are someone. And it's time you become that someone."

His faith is a cure. I can feel it heal my wounds, dissolve all my weakness.

"Boss."

A kid comes from the darkness. My fear stiffens me, but Shakes holds my hand, keeping me from fleeing.

My eyes keep on Shakes' face. He goes to the boy, slowly

releasing my hand from his own.

He had protected me with that bit of hold just then. Telling me not to run but to stay. And I stayed, knowing nothing of either person. I had somehow, at some time, put my trust in him.

A smile etches on my lips, and when Shakes comes back to me and holds out his hand, I don't hesitate to catch it. I'm lighter and freer than I have ever been since I could remember. I have hope creeping back into my heart.

I am going to become someone. I owe that much to Charles. I owe that much to myself.

33

Epilogue

I stand on the steps of Boundary overlooking the campus. Out of the light, the world is enveloped in darkness. Towers of shadows. There is evil here but it is not the kids. It's someone stronger, someone I've not yet met. The ones watching behind a screen, never interceding, enjoying the mayhem they've created. Like they've created me. It will be their biggest regret. I'm going to ignite the flame and set the world on fire. It's time I learn who I am and embrace the evil inside me.

Sirens wail like wolves howling in the night. It echoes, loud and piercing, an ominous signal of warning. I back step into Boundary, standing beside Shakes.

"You ready?" Excitement dances on his face.

"You have no idea."

Rules

Rule 1: Do Not Attempt Escape
   Rule 2: All Students Must Go To School
   Rule 3: Obey The Teachers
   Rule 4: Killing on School Grounds is Not Permitted
   Rule 5: No Violence While School is in Session
   Rule 6: Must Have a Permit to Possess a Gun
   Rule 7: Do Not Block Cameras
   Rule 8: Shipment is the Last Saturday of Every Month
   Rule 9: Harvest is the First Saturday of Every Month
   Rule 10: All New Recruits With Wrist Bands Must Participate in Harvest
   Rule 11: Reaping Will be the Second Friday of Every Month
   Rule 12: Snatchers Will Not be Harmed or Stopped
   Rule 13: Do Not Steal, Harm, or Lie to a Teacher or a Clan Member
   Rule 14: Do Not Pretend to be a Teacher or a Clan Member
   Rule 15: The Clan Coal Will Dispose of Waste
   Rule 16: The Clan Rain Will Provide Food and Water for the Populace.
   Rule 17: The Clan Boundary Will Guard The Wall
   Rule 18: The Clan Respect Will Enforce the Laws of the School.

Rule 19: Any Clanless Individual Will be Relocated
 *Punishment for Breaking the Rules Could Result in Expulsion

Rule 20: Anyone Found with Rebellious Intention Will be Immediately Executed.

My Name is Anarchy

Book 2
Available Now

What school doesn't have a little anarchy?
Ember—formally known as Scream—has joined Anarchy, a secret rebellion brewing under Myers' School for the Unwanted.. All that Anarchy requires from her is the memory she lost. But the insurmountable trauma of her past and her desire for revenge cloud her judgment, causing her to make grave mistakes that could cost Anarchy everything.

With time running out as Myers begins to hunt for her, Ember must find a way to remember…or forget about ever going home again.

Two percent of yearly sales of the Screams Series will be donated to The Human Trafficking Front.
If you or someone you know could be a victim, please call the National Center for Missing and Exploited Children at 1-800-843-5678

About the Author

Marissa Rivera is the author of Dystopian Thrillers like My Name is Scream. She was born in New Jersey but moved to Florida when she was a teenager with her mother who bought her a laptop to harness the magic of writing. When she is not working on her books, she busies herself with three needy kids and manages to stay sane with her goofball husband.

Please take the time to review work by Self-Publishing authors. Reviews are the life blood for their work. Thank you!

Find Marissa on Tiktok
  @authormarissarivera

Subscribe to my newsletter:
✉ http://marissarivera.net

Also by Marissa Rivera

Holy F*$&
Faye Gerald has always been the model student and the flawless daughter. When a meteor hits their small town of Georgia, Faye watches as all her dreams for a perfect future go up in flames. With the path home destroyed, Faye, her boyfriend, her best friend, and a boy she shouldn't know, journey down the mountainside to see if they can find anyone alive. But secrets travel with them and sometimes dreams have to come to an end.

Made in the USA
Middletown, DE
19 May 2023